"A PEARL BEYOND PRICE!"
HE WAS UPON HER IN
TWO STRIDES. . . .

The next instant she went crashing to the floor, felled by a vicious blow that left her stunned.

"Would you mar the face of such a beauty? Touch her again and you are dead!"

A second raider had charged into the room. Natia turned her head at the sound of his voice. He was elegantly garbed in silken robes banded from neck to hem with sable. Around his waist was a belt of hammered gold studded with enormous cabochon emeralds. Only a slaver could possess such jewels. She would be sold at auction to the highest bidder!

As if reading her thoughts, he shrugged. "You will bring a king's ransom on the block. Until then, your every move will be watched. It is useless to attempt escape. . . ."

Destiny's Bride

Lucy Phillips Stewart

A DELL BOOK

Published by
Dell Publishing Co., Inc.
1 Dag Hammarskjold Plaza
New York, New York 10017

Dell ® TM 681510, Dell Publishing Co., Inc.

ISBN: 0-440-12557-X

Printed in the United States of America

First printing—September 1979

Destiny's
Bride

CHAPTER ONE

Leaving the grassland behind, the horse entered upon a length of sandy beach which stretched for miles along the shore. At first glance one might write it down as a youth enjoying an early morning gallop, but a second glance would inevitably discover the swell of rounded breasts straining against a shirt of finest lawn, and the curve of feminine hips encased in breeches. In point of fact Natia had never scrupled to ride alone. From the age of eight it had become her custom to roam at will over her father's vast estates, attired in boy's clothing and unattended even by a groom.

Unknown to her, a tall gentleman mounted on a magnificent roan was observing her approach from his vantage point just off to the right. His smile grew, revealing a glimpse of excellent teeth, and he sent his horse angling toward her in long, bounding strides. Catching the movement out of the corner of her eye, Natia turned her head to look at him. There was nothing of the provincial in the cut of his coat, nor had the buckskins hugging his muscular thighs been fashioned by any local hand. She frankly stared.

Something of his intent must have communicated

itself to her; in sudden alarm she dug her heels into the mare's flanks, sending it thundering down the beach. Gradually the knowledge that her horse was no match for his obtruded, bringing an angry flush to her cheeks. One quick glance sufficed; she withdrew her gaze from the roan's silken nose inching forward at her elbow and addressed her attention to the not inconsiderable task of remaining astride her wildly galloping horse.

The length of the beach accomplished, she was obliged to draw the mare to a halt, and discovered the stranger much nearer at hand than she had hoped. He was, in fact, right beside her. A hateful smile curved his lips; she had no difficulty at all in interpreting the expression in his eyes.

"Magnificent," he said. "One can only envy the breeches."

Natia gasped and prepared to turn the mare about. His air of masculine superiority, indeed his whole aspect, filled her with loathing. His eyes were too blue, his nose too straight. His mouth, which was well-formed, seemed to sneer. She longed to slap him.

His voice brought her head around. "Who would have thought it," he remarked, his eyes running over her insolently. "A barque of frailty, in this of all imaginable places. I have absented myself too long."

Natia found her tongue at last. "Your return will no doubt bring joy to the village maidens," she shot back with all the sarcasm she could throw into her voice.

He burst out laughing. "But not to you," he chuckled, his gaze returning to her face. "I see I shall need to remedy that."

Before she realized his purpose his arm was around her, and she found herself being ruthlessly kissed. The instant he raised his head she dealt him one resounding blow full across the mouth with all the force at her command. His eyes narrowed, but he paid the blood on his lip no heed at all; his arm tightened around her, and she was pulled from the saddle, to hang dangling, clamped against his side. Uttering a furious protest, she attempted to wrench herself free, but her struggles only made him laugh. There was nothing gentle in his next kiss. She emerged from it outraged and shaken, more shaken than she dared admit.

She felt unable to bear the indignity of it and sought vainly in her mind for a remark sufficiently caustic to put him in his place. None occurred to her. "Put me down!" she said at last, fiercely. "If my husband were with me, you would not use me in this fashion!"

He looked first startled, then amused. "If you had a husband, my dear, you would not be riding abroad alone. Now don't mistake me. I like coming upon charmingly clad females—and unattended ones, at that."

She despised the flush rising in her cheeks, but nevertheless managed to put a great deal of scorn into her glance. "Even a dissolute such as yourself might remember the civility due a lady," she said, meeting his grin with a flaming look.

"Is it a lady, then?" he remarked, his eyes roaming to her breasts. "I thought it was a boy."

"Did you indeed?" she flashed, brows lifted in chilling hauteur. "Well, I'm not surprised at that. I doubt you number many ladies among your acquaintance."

He looked amused at this. "Not many," he agreed. "What is your name?"

It was so unexpected that she could only regard him with a questioning eye. "If you were a gentleman, sir, you would know not to ask," she said, thinking to rebuke him.

This reference to the appalling crudity of his conduct fell on deaf ears. "A mystery," he observed, not at all abashed. "Never mind, I daresay I shall soon discover it. I am not unknown in these parts."

Meeting the challenge in his eyes, and suspecting him capable of ferreting out the truth, she gave it up. "There is no need for you to bandy my name about," she told him, feeling foolish. "I am Lady Devon, of Devon Hall."

The effect of this revelation was not at all what she had expected. He gasped, his arm tightening about her convulsively. "The devil you say," he ejaculated, stunned.

A snide little smile curved her lips. Sensing that she had somehow acquired the upper hand, and having no idea why, she nevertheless savored her victory. Her triumph proved brief indeed; the next instant she found herself lowered somewhat roughly to the ground. She staggered, regained her balance, and met his glare unflinchingly. "Thank you," she said then with awful civility. "If you are quite finished, I will resume my ride."

He regarded her fixedly, his lips grim, before swinging down from his horse. "You will return to Devon Hall with me," he gritted, advancing on her with a purposeful stride.

Natia took a nervous step backward. "You may deem it a privilege, sir, but I most decidedly do not!" she informed him coldly.

He remained unmoved. "I deem it a damned nuisance," he shot back curtly.

Before she could realize his intent, he had plucked her off her feet and tossed her aboard the mare. She collapsed in the saddle in some disorder, righted herself, and thrust her feet into the stirrups. Up went her chin. "Why you think you can order me about in this high-handed fashion, I do not in the least know," she said, eyeing him with distinct disfavor.

He checked his movement to swing astride the roan, and looked at her across the horse's back. "You will," he said.

She met his look full. "I ride where I please and

with whom I please," she said in uncompromising accents.

For a perilous moment he hovered on the brink of losing his temper completely. Lips clamped together, he settled himself in his saddle and gathered up the reins. "Unless you wish to return home across my pommel, you will set your mount forward," he replied in just as uncompromising a tone.

She was taken aback, as much by the way in which he delivered his ultimatum as by his words. It occurred to her he was quite prepared to make good his threat. She controlled an impulse to give vent to the retort rising on her tongue, and rode off before him, preserving an icy front. To be obliged to bottle up her wrath at being taken for a hoyden (for which she admitted her breeches were to blame) without the satisfaction of throwing his own conduct in his teeth was so insupportable that she could not bring herself to look at him. No man before him had ever dared to kiss her.

The ride home seemed interminable before Devon Hall came into view and they arrived at the gates. Natia drew the mare to a halt. "I am perfectly capable of negotiating the drive without mishap," she said quietly, her eyes carefully straight ahead.

"I would presume so . . ." He paused, his gaze resting thoughtfully on her profile. "I'm afraid I have forgotten your Christian name."

She turned her head to look at him, feeling uncomfortable and thereby missing the implication of his words. "Pray, what concern is it of yours?" she asked him frankly.

His brows rose. "It has a familiar ring," he remarked, taking not the smallest notice of the coldness in her eyes. "There is one thing further. You will clothe yourself properly immediately you reach the house."

There came a prolonged silence. Natia was too much

surprised to take umbrage. "It is not for you to—my husband would raise no objection, I'm sure," she finished in a rush.

"Oh," he said. "I think you will find that he will."

Regretting having said so much, and having bid him a perfectly civil good-day, she set off down the drive, conscious of a feeling of exhilaration to which she could not give a name. Arrived, finally, in the seclusion of her own rooms, she found herself unable to put her by now very thoroughly disoriented thinking into any semblance approaching order. Surprisingly, she felt little alarm and no rage. More surprising still, she felt no regrets at having had her station in life mistaken. There was no blinking it; she had not found the stranger's kisses offensive, had come very close to responding. The admission brought a blush to her cheeks, and thoughts of her husband to her mind.

She was sure he had forgotten her very existence. She did not doubt it was his lawyers who had arranged for her passage from Russia, and certainly it was his man of business who had seen her established at Devon Hall and in the months since had made the arrangements that provided her with funds. She thought Lord Devon a very poor husband, but could not find it in her heart to blame him. It must be very disagreeable indeed to find oneself married to a girl young enough to be one's granddaughter. His lordship, she reflected, must be going on seventy years of age.

Her mother had spoken of him often, and of visiting Devon Hall as a child. When she had taken the idea into her head, there had been no reasoning with her. From the moment her husband met his untimely death, until her own, her daughter's future had consumed her every waking thought. Natia could understand this. Her father's heir had tolerated their presence in their former home, however grudgingly, but it was a tenuous situation at best, and one that could not continue on indefinitely. Her mother had realized this. Secluded on the estate, with no world beyond the Russian steppes, her thoughts had returned to her native England, and to the very person to have the care of her daughter in the event of her own demise. Once a marriage by proxy between Natia and Lord Devon occurred to the widow, there had been no stopping her. Her daughter would be provided for, her place in society secure. Despite any argument Natia could put forth, lengthy correspondence went back and forth, the papers were drawn up, and the thing was done. Gowned in white, and with her mother as witness, Natia had stood beside the proxy groom and repeated her vows. She felt no regrets. Her mother had died at peace. Only now, with the stranger's handsome face intruding in her thoughts, did she catch a glimpse of what her life might have been.

His parting words came to mind; she crossed the room to stand looking doubtfully at her reflection in the long mirror. It took no more than a cursory glance for her to admit that he was right. She looked much more a scrubby boy than the wife of a titled Englishman.

Her old Nurse came hurrying into the room and cast one hostile glare at the breeches. Natia would not have been surprised to be forced to endure a homily on a lady's proper regard for the conduct due her station, but Nurse had almost ceased to inveigh against her charge. Through the years she had learned that once Natia had made up her mind it was almost impossible to coax her out of doing whatever she chose. No one could describe Nurse as a linguist; she was prone to speak in fits and starts, the length of time it took her to come to the point revealing her state of agitation. The impatience with which Natia bore with her on this occasion was patent, but it was softened by her affection for the elderly woman, who had alternately petted her and remonstrated with her almost from the moment of her birth.

Gradually Nurse's disjointed utterances began to make sense. "Appear before his lordship in that garb, you will not!" she declared finally, in accents that clearly indicated she was prepared to stand her ground.

A look of astonishment crossed Natia's face. "Are you speaking of Lord Devon?" she asked, staring.

Nurse sniffed. "For all the notice he has paid you these many months, we may as well have been back in Russia. It was his lordship's valet—and I will say he at least seems civil—well, Missy, it was him as told me his master was in the house. Fine doings, I call it, not to have sent word ahead."

Natia sat down hard on a chair. "What is he like?— Lord Devon, I mean," she murmured in tones barely above a whisper.

"That, I couldn't say," Nurse replied. "Probably crusty. Most old gentlemen are."

"Pray don't say so," Natia groaned, looking anxious. "If only he isn't subject to gout!"

"Now don't you go borrowing trouble, Missy. You have enough of that as it is. Marston—his lordship's man—told me his lordship sent his compliments, and will be pleased if you will sup with him."

"Must I, Nettle?" Natia asked, gazing at Nurse with imploring eyes. "He will probably dine on bread and milk, and dribble it on his chin. I couldn't bear it."

"You will bear it. Not for nothing are you Count Smirnoff's daughter. Now you just get yourself out of that outlandish garb while I draw your bath. You are going downstairs dressed like the proper lady you are, make no mistake about it."

Nurse's bullying accomplished its healing effect. Promptly on the stroke of seven Natia descended the stairs, gowned in silver tulle over an underdress of satin, and with her mother's sapphires about her throat. The butler, much impressed, and bowing his head to hide it, begged her to follow him, and conducted her across the vast hall to a pair of mahogany doors leading into a small salon. Natia crossed the threshold, a welcoming smile on her lips, and stopped dead in her tracks. He was no longer wearing buckskins—indeed he was properly dressed for evening in a coat of emerald satin—but it was the tall gentleman of the earlier encounter. There could be no doubt. Natia stared in blank astonishment, totally bereft of speech.

He gave no sign of having noticed. "I felicitate you on your appearance," he said, lifting her fingers to his lips. "It is much improved."

Natia found her tongue suddenly. "What are you doing here?" she demanded, an angry flush mounting in her cheeks.

His eyes narrowed. "Whom did you expect?" he said.

"My husband, of course."

"I am afraid you are laboring under some misapprehension. I am Lord Devon."

Natia fairly gaped. "But, you aren't old," she said in a great deal of bewilderment. "Lord Devon is—quite elderly."

He shrugged. "No doubt you are referring to my grandfather," he said. "I trust you will find me acceptable in his stead."

Natia found it difficult to take in what he had said, or even to think clearly. In a voice that didn't seem to belong to her, she said, "But surely you aren't—you can't be—I m-married—"

"You married me," he replied, his penetrating gaze resting on her flushed face. "My grandfather was ill at the time he first agreed to the—match. Unfortunately, by the time the papers had been drawn up, he knew he would be dead by the time the ceremony had taken place in Russia. Since it was too late to retract, he requested I take his place."

It was like a bad dream, a nightmare in which one tried to escape from some horrible doom, only to find oneself powerless to flee. Raising piteous eyes, she said, clutching at straws, "The papers named his lordship—your grandfather—"

"My grandfather and I bore the same name. It was all quite legal, believe me."

She felt as if she wanted to cry. But she didn't cry. She said, simply, "I refuse to believe you."

He knit his brows. "Possibly you do, but it doesn't alter the fact. You will do better to accept it."

She did not reply, for she could think of nothing it was possible to say. Instinctively she knew that what he said was true. An elderly gentleman would have accorded her the courtesy of his acquaintance the instant she set foot on English soil, scant comfort at the moment. A thought occurred to her. She said a faint flush tinging her cheeks with pink, "Will you tell me why you did it?"

His reply was brief. "I had no choice," he said. "My honor was at stake."

"I have never heard of anything so ridiculous!" she exclaimed, startled. "What if you should one day wish to marry?"

"I will not, I hope, find myself confronted with that problem." He added, with the glimmer of a smile, "I trust that the longevity which runs in my family also runs in yours?"

Natia felt much inclined to think him mad. "This is insupportable," she said, glancing away. "Something must be done. I will apply for a divorce."

He stiffened. "Never speak to me of divorce!" he said, his mouth grim. "No Devon has thought to drag our name through a scandal in the courts. You may find the idea distressing, but you are married to me, and married you will stay!"

Natia, who had been listening to this speech in growing anger, met the awesome stare of his blue eyes with a fierce glare of her brown ones. "Very well," she said in tones far from humbled, "but I will inform you, sir, if you are contemplating kissing me again, you may forget it."

"By all means," he agreed, composing his features. "As a matter of fact, I am not contemplating it."

"Oh!" she said, dashed.

His smile gleamed. "We will be leaving for London before many days," he said. "In the meantime, shall we agree to—coexist in peace?"

She looked him full in the face. "I think we should go our separate ways, my lord. In fact, I'm sure of it. You know as well as I that you cannot just reappear with a bride on your arm and expect anyone to believe it. They wouldn't, you know."

"You would like remaining here alone, wouldn't you?" he said after a moment's pause, his eyes on her golden curls. "There would be no one left to spoil your idyll."

"Why should you say that?" she inquired, her brows knit. "It is as if you wish to think the worst of me."

"No, I'm trying to talk some sense into your head. You may think yourself isolated here at Devon Hall, but it would only be a matter of time before someone found you out. I shan't risk it."

She flushed, but replied with dignity, "I will instruct my maid to stand in readiness to pack."

"I trust you will also instruct her to burn your breeches?"

The breath caught in her throat. She said, with an edge in her voice, "If you took a disgust of me, I wonder you should not return to London alone."

"It had been my original intent," he replied, preserving his calm. "Seeing you, I changed my mind. I shouldn't be surprised if I had sought you out earlier, had I known."

"No doubt I should be grateful for your notice—however tardily given."

"I meant it for a compliment. Do you imagine I think you plain? I don't." His smile flashed. "Even in breeches," he added, explaining himself.

"It is to be hoped," she said with strong feeling, "that I am not destined to spend an excess of time in your company. You seem to delight in goading me."

Amusement gleamed in his eyes. "Don't tell me you dislike crossing swords with me. I know better."

"How can you be so odious?" she demanded in biting accents. "You have as good as accused me of inveigling you into marriage, and I very much resent it."

"I haven't done any such thing," he replied mildly. "I merely explained how it came about. Come now, don't scowl at me. I have no wish to bicker."

"Yes, you have," she contradicted him. "In fact, you not only give voice to whatever comes into your head, you—well, you will admit you mauled me abominably."

"Now, that will never do," he remarked, amused. "You can have no notion of what a mauling entails, if you think that."

Her lips tightened. "You may be sure I find your sense of humor insufferable," she said in scathing accents. "And what's more, I'm much inclined to think I dislike you excessively."

A muscle twitched at the corner of his lips. "Being innocent of voicing whatever comes into your own mind must be a comfort," he said with a perfectly straight face.

A startled expression crossed her face. "I'm afraid I deserved that," she admitted, stung. "How persistent you are. I should think you would permit me an occasional lapse."

"If you wish it," he agreed with marked politeness.

She eyed him doubtfully. "I cannot conceive that we are all suited," she said, then hastened to add, "Not that either of us expects—or thinks— Oh, dear!"

"Why aren't we suited?" he promptly demanded.

"For one thing, you are English, while I'm Russian."

"Half Russian. What else?"

"I know little of the social world, except for an occasional trip to St. Petersburg. Mama and Papa preferred the country. So you see, I'm not at all up to snuff."

"It won't wash, you know. Society may be foolish, but it isn't blind. It will be charmed."

Natia felt the flush creeping into her cheeks. She knew he was flattering her, but she was not used to receiving compliments. Only her father had called her pretty.

He had crossed to hold open the door for her to precede him to the dining room. Without giving him another glance, she walked past him and across the hall, the sense of struggling with forces beyond her control sweeping over her. It did not seem to her that she could bear the domesticity of the scene. She was trapped, not in marriage with an elderly acquaintance of her mother, but with a young and virile man. She frowned, and tried to steer her mind sharply away from the thought.

To her surprise, a variety of dishes were set out upon the table, more, in fact, than she had before seen assembled together at one time. More surprising still, no servants stood waiting respectfully to serve them. She went slowly forward and took the chair he was holding for her, feeling slightly revolted by the sight of so much food.

Apparently he felt the same, for he looked up from the soup he was ladling into her bowl and said,

"After we have made our selection, I will send the remainder to the kitchens."

"You will do better to send your compliments," she instantly responded. "Cook must have been hard pressed to dress so many dishes in—well, in honor of your return."

His brows shot up. "Does that mean you think his talents could have been employed to better purpose?"

"Perhaps," she said.

He gave a shout of laughter. "Tell me," he said. "Do you hold all men in dislike, or is it only I?"

She regarded him silently for a moment. "As to that," she said finally, "I couldn't say. I met few gentlemen on the Russian steppes."

"The Cossacks must be blind," he remarked. "Tell me about your life."

"There isn't much to tell. At least, nothing that would interest you."

"Suppose you let me judge that for myself."

"I passed all my life at home. There is nothing to be said of that. I would much rather hear about you, Lord Devon."

His eyes were on her face in a way that was hard to read. "My name is Colin," he said. "Colin Fortas Devereau, to be exact."

Her eyes began to dance. "Well, unless you take exception to it, I'm sure I have no objection. I can't think why."

He saw the humor of it and smiled. "The least you can do in return is to identify yourself."

"My name is Natia," she replied, looking startled. "Don't you find it strange you shouldn't know?"

"I hesitate to bruise your ego, but it had slipped my mind. No, don't fire up at me. You may be comforted by the knowledge that I read the marriage contract."

"Then you know you are to provide me with an abode?"

"I have provided you with no less than three abodes, my dear."

"In the first place, my lord, I am not your dear. In the second, I understood the contract called for separate housing."

"Undoubtedly you did. In that particular, however, the wording was somewhat vague."

She stared at him in blank astonishment and said, "Surely you aren't suggesting—when you said we go to London, naturally I assumed you would rent a place for me!"

His glance swept her face. "Certainly not," he said.

She felt her brain to be reeling. "But you—you cannot mean you expect to share a—a house with me?" she gasped, appalled.

"I am much afraid I do," he said.

"But—Oh, there is some mistake!" she cried. "Mama didn't intend I should l-live with you!"

"Your mother," he explained, "placed you in the care of Lord Devon. I need not remind you that I am he."

An unladylike expression escaped her lips. "Of course," she agreed. "There is no denying that."

He studied her briefly. "Do rid yourself of the notions that are revolving through your pretty head," he said. "I have no desire to share your bed."

That drew a surprised gasp from her, and words he hadn't expected to hear from her lips. "My life up to now may have been horribly restricted," she said, "but I know precisely what you mean. Well, sir, it wasn't my intention to discuss it, but now that you have brought the subject up, I will say that you may have as many mistresses as you wish, provided you are discreet. I presume you have—"

His lips twitched, once he recovered from the shock. "Not at the moment," he said.

"You will," she replied, quite obviously pleased.

Slightly taken aback, it was his turn to frown. "I seem to be more than ordinarily dull-witted this evening, but—I don't take your meaning."

Natia, watching his expression closely, said abruptly, "You wouldn't care to have a wife interfering in your affairs. I understand that perfectly, and will engage not to do so."

The corners of his lips quivered. "In that case," he replied, "it is fortunate that I married you. Few wives would be so magnanimous."

She shot him a suspicious look. "Is it a bargain, then?" she asked, and waited breathlessly for his reply.

"I am beginning to think that it is," he said, looking at her rather enigmatically. "Am I permitted to ask what you intend doing in return?"

"But I've already told you," she replied, bewildered. "I will be a docile wife, so long as you—"

"So long as I seek my creature comfort elsewhere," he finished for her.

She flushed to the roots of her hair. "Since we understand one another, we should deal famously together," she said. "And now, if you don't mind, I would like to change the subject."

"I have been waiting for us to do so," he replied, truthfully. "It is fortunate that I had the foresight to dismiss the servants for our first evening alone together."

"You must have been worried I would say something to embarrass you," she said, stung.

"Not worried," said his lordship. "Omniscient, perhaps."

CHAPTER TWO

The arrival of Lord Devon's relatives some three days later was witnessed by Natia from the sanctuary of her room. The sound of wheels crunching on gravel in the courtyard below failed to attract her attention until it became apparent an equipage was drawing up before the door. She flew across to a window and stood gazing down upon a scene that was certainly impressive. Four perfectly matched grays were harnessed to a coach with a crest upon its panel. Two outriders accompanied it, while drawn up behind it was a second vehicle with a mountain of baggage piled high atop its roof. The steps of the coach were let down, the door was opened, and a gentleman stepped down.

Although only twenty-nine years of age, Lord Devon's brother-in-law was sadly inclined to fat. His countenance, without being handsome, was by no means displeasing. He had a decided air of fashion, and if he found it necessary to squeeze his girth into tight stays to adopt a certain extravagance of dress, at least his corset did not creak when he moved.

He was followed from the coach a moment later by a pretty female of great elegance and propriety. She

was dressed in the prevailing mode in a high-waisted
dress with tiny puff-sleeves, a fashion which became
her very well. There was a great deal of decision in
her gray eyes, and if she was sometimes inclined to
speak succinctly when dealing with her husband, he
was far too indolent to assert himself.

By the time the third member of the party was
ready to descend, the butler had trod sedately down
the front steps with his attendant satellites to assist
her to alight. A jewel case, a parasol, and two bags
containing the perfumes and lotions without which
their owner seldom ventured from her home were given
into the keeping of the grooms, and the Dowager Lady
Devon herself descended. A widow of many years standing, she enjoyed excellent health. When young she
had been a ruling toast; in middle age she retained
enough of her former beauty to be envied by the less
fortunate among her acquaintance. Like her daughter
she had the figure for the fashion in dress first in-
troduced by the Empress Josephine of France, called
the Empire mode, but unlike her daughter, who sometimes donned dresses which clung revealingly to her
body, the widow eschewed low-cut bodices and clinging gowns.

Natia, meanwhile, standing as though rooted before
her window, had realized the identity of the new
arrivals. Devon resembled his mother closely, while
the other lady could only be his sister. All three of
them shared the same classic profile, and if the widow's
dark hair displayed some few strands of gray, it had
once been as raven as her offsprings'. Natia felt dazed,
the privacy she had clung to since Devon first appeared upon the scene vanishing with the entry of his
relations into the house. She could now expect to be
thrown much more into his lordship's company. Overcome, it was some moments before she could recollect
herself enough to sit down to await a summons from
below.

The visitors, meanwhile, ushered by the butler into the green salon, declined all offers of refreshment and disposed themselves about the room while a groom went in search of Lord Devon. It would perhaps be more accurate to say that Lady Sherwood and the Dowager Lady Devon disposed themselves. Lord Sherwood took the seat indicated to him by his wife. Sitting down, he said mildly, "I still think we should have alerted Devon that we were coming."

His wife cast him a reproving look. "We have been over that before, Thomas. I cannot think why you should imagine we aren't welcome in Colin's home."

"Why should we be? The man's only newly married, remember. You can't expect him to relish having a pack of relations turn up on his doorstep. I'm sure I wouldn't."

The widow, who had seldom given a thought to the actions of her children, nevertheless could not think of the possibility her son had married without suffering the pangs of frustration. It was not, as might have been supposed by the look of indignation she directed at Thomas, that she mourned the loss of a son. She had, in the years since her children had grown to adulthood, enjoyed untrammeled freedom and a sizeable jointure which enabled her to indulge any extravagant whim that took her fancy. However much she might have anticipated her son's eventual marriage, it was not to be expected that she could bear with equanimity his alleged espousing of a bride not of her own choosing, and a proxy one at that. She had, in fact, long before settled on the very girl for him. It was to this that she referred now. "I cannot conceive that he could have taken a nobody to wife, and a foreigner into the bargain! When I think of Alice Elspin, and her Papa's thousands—"

Lorinda, who had listened repeatedly to her mother's lament during the days just past, did not in the least grudge her brother the privilege of choosing his own bride. Alice Elspin seemed to her an insipid chit, Earl's daughter or not. "It doesn't signify speaking of it, Mama," she replied, stripping off her gloves. "I'm sure the girl will turn out to be presentable. Thomas will agree, I know."

Thomas, with two sets of eyes on him, one pair in expectation, the other in disapproval, attempted to straddle the fence. "Entirely presentable, my love," he said. "Unless she squints."

Lorinda gasped. "Thomas!" she cried, scandalized. "Colin never would!"

Lady Devon cast her eyes heavenward. "You both know I have never interfered in his affairs," she began with a supreme disregard for the truth, "but it had been an understood thing that Lady Alice would be his choice. I don't know how we can face the child."

"You mean the Earl," Lorinda corrected her. "We cannot let that signify, Mama. This girl Colin married—I understand she is of respectable lineage."

"Respectable lineage!" Thomas repeated, goggling. "If that don't beat all! Her father was a Russian—some outlandish name—but he was a Count. That should be respectable enough for you!"

The next instant he found himself the target of his wife's scorching tongue, his mother-in-law having sought recourse in her vinaigrette. "I hope, Thomas," Lorinda said in biting accents, "that you do not mean to imply any disparagement against my family name!"

"I never thought of such a thing," he gasped, appalled. "Don't set your feathers up. I'm sure there is no better name in England. It's just that, well, since Colin has married the chit, we may as well accept it. For myself, I'm prepared to like her."

A vision of her brother crossed Lorinda's mind. "Yes," she agreed. "So am I."

Lady Devon fumbled for her hartshorn. "Unnatural daughter," she uttered in failing accents. "Here the family is at an end, and you don't seem to care. I cannot see what I have done to deserve this. For myself, I do not mind. I am thinking of your children."

Loyalty to Colin forced Lorinda to say, "Now, Mama," in pleading accents. "I don't think it will come to that."

"That is all very well for you to say, but I know how society will react. I have lived in dread of him taking up with some frightful creature. It would create a scandal, but that would pass. A low-born mistress is one thing; a wife of questionable background is something else entirely! Why, oh why, could he not have married some eligible girl years ago!"

"All they wanted was his money," Thomas offered tentatively.

"What does that signify, pray?" Lady Devon demanded.

A voice speaking from the doorway brought their heads around. "A great deal, ma'am," Lord Devon remarked, strolling forward to bow with languid grace over the hand she held out to him. "I trust I find you well?"

"It is surprising that you do," she replied, loosening the strings of her reticule and groping in it for a letter. "Explain this, if you please."

Devon took it from her hand and spread it open. "It seems quite clear to me," he said. "What do you wish explained?"

"I am aware one of your horrid lawyers penned these odious lines," she replied, indicating the letter with the stab of a finger, "but I had hoped to hear you deny them. Surely you cannot have entered into a marriage by proxy with a foreigner!"

"You will see it differently after you have made Natia's acquaintance," he said in a perfectly grave voice. "She should be down soon. I sent word to her the moment I was informed of your arrival."

His reply surprised no one, least of all his mother.

They all knew he had adored his grandfather; Lady Devon herself had felt quite the opposite. She said, in a peevish voice, "I cannot conceive what should have induced you to accede to that disagreeable old man's demands. He was ever a tyrant, with no thought for anyone's wishes but his own."

"There is no understanding it," Lorinda agreed. "To have tied yourself for life—"

"Oh, I say, m'dear," Thomas interposed, "this won't do. It won't do at all. It's Colin's business, 'pon my soul it is."

A humorous gleam came into Devon's eyes. "You comfort me, Thomas," he said.

Thomas extended his luck so far as to laugh. A moment later he found himself the recipient of a quelling look directed his way by Lady Devon. "I hope," she said, "you are not suggesting that Lorinda and I have no stake in this shocking affair. It will be up to us to put a brave face on it to the world. The last thing we need is questionable behavior on your part."

There came a pause. Thomas, glancing at Devon, hastily averted his eyes from the grimness he read in his brother-in-law's face. Surprising everyone, in cluding himself, he said, "I don't intend Colin should be subjected to such talk in his own house. What's more, we shouldn't be here. I never wanted to come, don't forget."

"Thomas!" Lorinda gasped. "Whatever has come over you!"

"He must have taken leave of his senses," Lady Devon added. "I'm sure he thinks to provoke us."

"I mean exactly what I say," Thomas asserted, emboldened by the supportive presence of a second male. "A man marries where he will. You can't call this— this Natia—an undesirable female. You know nothing about her."

"Nonsense!" Lady Devon snapped. "We know all we need to know."

A pained silence followed this remark. Devon was gazing at the carpet beneath his feet, the lids veiling his eyes. "To be plain with you," he said, looking up, "I haven't sought your approval."

Lorinda studied him thoughtfully. "Are you in love with her?" she demanded suddenly.

"I am not."

"Then what has put you on the defensive?"

"I must be remarkably obtuse," he replied, his eyes dwelling inscrutably upon her face.

Lorinda bridled. "You know to a nicety what I mean. If your emotions were involved, there would be no more to be said. But since they aren't, why, pray, should you turn disdainful?"

"Ah, but you see," he said, "I had every right to expect my family would close ranks behind me."

The Dowager Lady Devon sighed audibly and asked what she had done to deserve spending her declining years sunk in mortification. Since she customarily sought sympathy with such laments, Lorinda ignored the remark, saying that for herself she was prepared to introduce Natia into society.

A vision of the social season spent in the company of his relations crossed Devon's mind. "I would not dream of putting you to the trouble," he said, the lids veiling his eyes again.

"Do not suppose that you could bring Natia into good order with the ton without our help," Lorinda replied somewhat tartly. "There is no denying that few people have seen fit to withhold their approval of whatever you chose to do in the past, but if you will only consider it, you will know that in this instance I am right."

"You are very obliging," he remarked, a faint sneer curving his lips. "To put it bluntly, I lack sufficient credit myself to pull it off alone."

"Do not let us beat about the bush, Colin. Your activities over the past two years are well known to us. I imagine I need not point out to you that the world of fisticuffs and curricle-racing is far removed from the world of fashion. Unless you wish your wife to exist upon the fringes of society, you will leave it in our hands."

"I wonder if I shall?" he replied, smiling faintly.

"I should think it advisable," she responded, coloring slightly. "However much we might deprecate this strange marriage of yours, I hope we see our duty clear."

A silence fell with this remark, broken only by a slight sound from the doorway as Natia crossed the threshold and advanced hesitantly into the room. She was met with startled stares not wholly explained by her unheralded appearance upon the scene. Devon, mentally cursing the butler for not alerting him by announcing her arrival, and wondering how much of the conversation she had overheard, left his place before the fire to lead her forward. Natia curtsied silently as each introduction was made, speech seemingly beyond her powers at the moment. They all then stood rather awkwardly until Lord Sherwood delivered himself of obviously rehearsed, and somewhat ponderous, words of welcome. Natia hazarded from this outburst that his lordship may have defied his wife's injunctions to remain aloof, and it no doubt followed that the Dowager Lady Devon must harbor the same sentiments as her daughter. Devon himself would have been much relieved to know this was merely conjecture on her part and not, as he feared, a result of eavesdropping. Not that it mattered. Natia would have been insensitive indeed not to notice the coolness which permeated the room. For her part, she found the interview decidedly painful, but she would neither display her discomfiture nor allow the conversation to lag.

Devon, she felt, conducted himself just as he ought. He addressed himself most particularly to her, and if there was a faint bitterness in his tone at times, it soon become apparent that it was his relatives' behavior of which he disapproved. They relentlessly cross-examined her on her antecedents and seemed unwilling to accept her replies as fact. When, finally, they rose to seek their rooms, she made no effort to detain them. There was nothing she could say. Devon realized this and did not embarrass her with apologies. He offered her his arm, and after a slight hesitation she laid her hand on it and allowed him to escort her to her rooms.

Not altogether to Natia's surprise, if to her chagrin, the guests' stay became prolonged. Originally intending to remain for some four weeks, their eighth week had come and gone and still they tarried. Natia could only find consolation in the thought that it could not go on forever. Each day's post was quickly scanned in hope that a letter addressed to one or another of them would be found among the stack delivered to the door. They did receive mail, but she could only conclude that no missile among the many was of a nature to cause them to return home.

The atmosphere at Devon Hall could not be termed harmonious. There had in fact been numerous distressing scenes, and one in particular, when the Dowager had delivered herself of several caustic remarks directed at Natia's bowed head, which Natia would have preferred not to remember. For a perilous moment she had feared Devon might seize his mother and shake her, but he found enough control to seize her arm instead and hustle her from the room. She could only imagine what transpired at a later meeting between the two, for the Dowager, in the privacy of her rooms, had enjoyed one of her more interesting spasms. All this Natia learned from Nettle, though

she stopped short of allowing her old Nurse to indulge in agreeable speculations.

It was not very long after this episode that Devon
put forth his determination to remove to London,
the start of the social season being close at hand.
Natia, though momentarily cast down, soon consoled
herself with the reflection that the loss of her early
morning gallop was a small price to pay for freedom
from her new relations. The intelligence, however,
that the Dowager and Lady Sherwood intended being
very much a part of her debut soon put an end to any
happy musings. She attempted to decline their services
politely, and struggled to restore her composure when
she found it would not serve.

"We will need to undertake the task of your entrée
into the world with a great deal of care," the Dowager
remarked one evening following dinner, the ladies
having withdrawn from the dining room to the small
salon, leaving the gentlemen to their port. "Society's
decision cannot be expected to be in your favor if you
have no background to recommend you."

"Oh?" Natia said, with an edge in her voice.

"My advice to you," the Dowager continued, "is to
put yourself unreservedly in our hands. Do not make
the mistake of thinking Devon's title sufficient to open
all doors to you. You will need an acceptable family
history if our plans are to meet with any measure of
success. Is it too much to hope your mother came of
good stock?"

It was too much for Natia to swallow. "I should
think my father's title equal to Devon's own," she
said, rising to her feet in one graceful movement.

"A Russian Count about whom no one has heard?"
the Dowager snorted in derision. "Pray, do not be
absurd."

Natia blushed to the roots of her hair. "You will, if
you please, refrain from insulting me with remarks
in that vein," she replied in a withering tone.

The Dowager caught her breath on a gasp. "Do not suppose yourself alone in having been laid open to insult," she said in equally chilling accents.

Natia instantly regretted having allowed her unruly tongue to betray her into speaking rudely, however well-deserved her words. "If you will excuse me, I have the headache," she said, dropping a curtsy before turning and swiftly crossing to the door.

She hurried up the stairs, and in the seclusion of her room gave Nurse a highly emotional account of the confrontation. By the time she arrived at the end of her tale, Nurse was justly incensed, but not enough to heed her instruction to pack a valise. "And where do you plan to go at this hour of the night?" she inquired in a reasoning tone.

"It doesn't matter," Natia replied, distraught. "Surely you must realize I cannot stand much more of this odious persecution!"

"You said much the same back in Russia before you agreed to marry Lord Devon," Nurse pointed out.

"But this is different!" Natia cried, a sob in her throat. "I have been continually on trial here, and Devon has had nothing to say in my defense. You know that as well as I!"

"How could he?" Nurse demanded, bewildered. "You have avoided his company at every turn. I doubt you have seen him alone above twice in all the time he has been in the house. You may be sure his Mama knows this, Missy."

Natia turned astonished eyes toward Nurse. "How can you, Nettle!" she exclaimed. "It is as if you would put the blame on me!"

"I am only saying you haven't given his lordship a chance—"

"Understand this, Nettle!" Natia interrupted. "I will *not* remain here under any circumstances whatsoever, least of all in the company of people who insult me at every turn. I am amazed you would sanction it, but that is neither here nor there. I have thought it out and I am returning to Russia. You may come with me or stay behind; it is up to you."

Nurse had been too many years in service to Natia to argue further. "Very well," she said, "but we will not go running off on some wild goose chase without first making plans. We will need transport across the Channel—or better still, all the way to Greece. With that Bonaparte person loose in Europe, it wouldn't be safe, going by land."

Natia uttered a tinkling laugh. "You may be trying to hoax me," she said, "but I know why you are being so obliging. You are homesick for the steppes."

Nurse looked at the glowing countenance turned to her and said simply: "My home is where you are, Missy."

"Yes, I know," Natia replied in a shaken voice. "Whatever would I do without you, Nettle?"

Nurse suddenly became busy rearranging the bottles of perfumes and lotions on Natia's dressing table. "The stagecoach office in Dawlish will furnish me with direction to Exeter," she said. "I imagine an ill relative will provide a reason for my going there. It's a matter of money, Missy. Have we enough to purchase our passage on a packet bound for home?"

Natia flew across to a chest against the wall and pulled open a drawer. "Thank goodness I have had scant opportunity to spend my allowance," she said, lifting out a bag heavy with gold coins. "We have more than enough for our purpose."

Nurse poured out a handful of the sovereigns. "You will need outmoded gowns and serviceable boots if we are to divert attention from your station," she murmured, tipping a further coin into her palm. "We will pass you off as my daughter."

Natia gazed at her, fascinated. "I must say you think of everything," she said admiringly.

"If I had a grain of common sense, I wouldn't fall

in with your harebrained schemes," Nurse replied, frowning. "What if Count Sergei refuses you admittance when—and if—we finally arrive in Russia?"

"He won't," Natia said with more assurance than she felt. "He may have been Papa's heir, but it was my home too, remember. I would rather be unwelcome there, than here."

Nurse turned thoughtful eyes on her charge. "There is one thing, Missy. Did Count Sergei ever cast out lures to you?"

Natia's tinkling laugh rang out again. "Don't be a goose," she said. "When he marries, he will make a splendid match. You needn't worry he will wish to make me the object of his gallantry. I'm not only penniless, I'm already married."

Nurse curbed a strong desire to remark further upon the baser inclinations of the male. "Very likely he won't," she contented herself with saying, and went away to lay out Natia's nightgown and turn back her bed.

It was nearly an hour later, when Natia was drifting off to sleep, that a rap sounded on the door and Devon strode purposefully into the room. She quickly drew the sheet up under her chin, but he caught a glimpse of rounded breasts beneath a gown of filmiest gauze, and drew in his breath. The only consolation which afforded her some slight degree of satisfaction was his obvious discomfiture, as evidenced by the flush creeping into his cheeks.

"What are you doing in my room?" she demanded, bunching her muscles to flee should he advance toward her.

"I have several reasons," he responded, leaning his broad shoulders against the bedpost.

"No!" she said, clutching the sheet tighter still.

A sardonic gleam came into his eyes. "Rid yourself of the notion that I cherish designs upon your person," he said, folding his arms across his chest. "It is not my custom to force my attention upon unwilling females."

"Very likely it isn't," she replied with a touch of asperity. "The females you have known would have been most cooperative, I make no doubt. Perhaps you will permit me to tell you I consider you positively rag-mannered to come bursting into my chamber unannounced!"

"Which leaves me to suppose you are accustomed to gentlemen entering your chamber by invitation," he remarked provocatively.

She shot him a murderous look. "Your imagination does run away with you, doesn't it?" she said disdainfully. "Well, you may curb it, sir. No gentleman before you has been so bold."

"I didn't think one had," came his maddening reply.

"Oh!" she stormed. "I must say I find this conversation most improper!"

"It has taken the direction decreed by you, my girl, so don't talk balderdash to me," he replied, pushing his shoulders away from the post. "Good God! I hope you have too much sense to think you have aught to fear from me!"

"What in the world makes you think I fear you?" she asked with a great deal of bravado.

He moved to the side of the bed and stood looking down at her, frowning slightly. "Enough of this," he said. "I came to inform you that we leave for London in a fortnight."

She glanced at his face and swiftly looked away. "Your mother will be glad of that, I should think," she replied, only hoping that her eyes had not betrayed the dismay his words had brought.

"Doubtless she will, but as it happens her sentiments upon this occasion do not concern me. I have had a talk with her. She will be staying with us during the coming weeks, but only to introduce you to society. Pay no heed to her tongue. She doesn't mean half the things she says."

She raised her brows. "I imagine she does," she said.

His eyes flashed. "I acknowledge that you have every night to suppose that, but I had flattered myself into thinking you had come to hold me in some esteem. I don't deny you had reason for grievance at our first meeting, but I should be grateful if you will cease flinging it in my teeth!"

"In that case, I must assuredly do so," she said with a faintly mocking little smile.

"Oh, for God's sake!" he said explosively. "Can't you act sensibly for once!"

She was spared the necessity of answering by Nurse's sudden appearance upon the scene. "What is all this hubbub, Missy?" she demanded, hurrying into the room. "I must say—Oh!" she finished on a gasp, catching sight of Lord Devon standing beside Natia's bed.

Natia had been fast approaching a state of seething fury, but the dumbfounded expression on Nurse's face turned wrath into amusement. "I am perfectly safe, Nettle," she said. "Lord Devon is just on the point of leaving."

"Well, in that case—" Nurse muttered, eyeing his lordship suspiciously. "If you are sure—"

A thunderous look came upon Devon's face. "Out!" he commanded, controlling his spleen with obvious effort.

"Nettle, pray, do go," Natia hastened to add. "There is no cause for concern. His lordship only came to speak privately to me about his plans."

Nurse reluctantly turned away. "If you need me, I will be just outside," she said, closing the door behind her with a snap.

Devon's attention became focused upon Natia. "You may as well know I don't intend a servant questioning my presence in your bedroom," he said. "You may hold me at arm's length, but your maid shan't engage to do so!"

This blunt reference to his right to be there brought a flush into her cheeks. "It would certainly be carrying her duty to excess," she managed to say. "There's no saying, however, what she might do if she found you here again."

The absurdity of it struck him. He smiled and took her hands in his. "I don't mean to succumb to your suggestion," he said. "You have convinced yourself that you prefer to sleep alone since you find that infinitely preferable to thoughts of sleeping with me. But it won't serve, you know. You aren't indifferent to me. You haven't been from the first time I kissed you."

"No—oh, no!" she said, striving to remove her fingers from his grasp. "Don't speak so!"

"You may think that I am indifferent in my turn, but I'm not," he replied, smiling into her eyes. "It won't be easy, but I promise not to force you."

Something between panic and hysteria seized her, panic because his meaning had become very clear to her, and hysteria because she knew she lacked the strength to oppose him. She could only stare numbly while he raised her fingers to his lips and kissed them before going out of the room without another word.

Nurse immediately came back in and cast Natia one swift, searching look. "I don't suppose it was improper, Missy," she said. "Imprudent, more like."

"I know that!" Natia returned crossly. "Don't fuss. We have more pressing matters on our minds. You must arrange our passage tomorrow, or the day after at the latest. We must be away from here well before a fortnight passes. Otherwise I will be hustled off to London and the opportunity will be lost."

"Perhaps that would suit our purpose just as well."

"I think not, Nettle. If we leave from here, his lordship won't bother to pursue me. But I have an idea his pride would force him to do so if his London friends knew of it."

CHAPTER THREE

Nurse, on whom the decision to return to Russia had acted like a strong tonic, went to Dawlish on the next market day and spent an agreeable hour browsing among the stalls set up along the town's principal thoughfare. Coming away with two serviceable cambric gowns and a plain cloak of twilled sarcenet, she felt well satisfied that Natia would be dressed appropriately for their journey, if not in the first style of fashion. But upon her return to Devon Hall, and upon perceiving the loathsome way in which Natia eyed the purchases, she found it expedient to say, with a touch of authority, that such attire was necessary to remove from their appearance any flavor of the Quality. Natia submitted, therefore, only extracting a promise that Nurse would pack one fashionable gown for her initial appearance before her relatives in Russia.

In all the decisions preparatory to their leaving, Natia bowed to Nurse's judgment: they would each travel with one valise, that being the amount of luggage Nurse deemed it possible to manage without assistance; they would travel with their money sewn into the hem of Nurse's gown, as a precaution against footpads; and in the meantime Natia would turn a sweet face upon Lord Devon, lest he become suspicious and frustrate all their plans. Natia spent the two days before their departure in an agony of dread, but nothing occurred to thwart their schemes. They arose at a very early hour on the morning of the third day, slipped from the house unobserved (or so they thought), and began the long trek to the King's Arms Inn in Dawlish, to catch the stage to Exeter.

The weather had turned raw by the time the Accommodation coach pulled out of the courtyard of the inn. A light rain had fallen throughout the night, leaving puddles in the road which hid the chuckholes from the coachman's view. From the muttering issuing from his throat, it seemed probable that the young guard seated by his side would add a certain salty color to his own expanding vocabulary. The pace was necessarily slow, but even so the cumbersome vehicle bounced and jostled over the ruts and potholes, threatening to unseat the two hardy gentlemen clinging to their seats upon the roof, and tossing the inside passengers about unmercifully. In addition to Natia and Nurse, these latter consisted of a jovial man wrapped to his ears in a muffler, and a rawboned countrywoman with a hamper of food on the floor between her feet. Upon the initial start of the journey, the gentleman had addressed a remark to Natia, only to encounter Nurse's frigid stare. He had indulged in no further conversation.

By the time they reached Starcross, the rain had begun to fall, lightly at first, and then in torrents. The horses labored on, their hooves slipping in the mud, but the coach was making slow progress. The countrywoman wrapped her shawl more closely about her shoulders and said she had known from the outset they would never reach their destination on time. The gentleman was much too occupied in keeping his muffler in place to vouchsafe a reply, but Natia prophesied the downpour must soon abate, a remark which seemed to afford the woman scant comfort.

Past Kenton the rain did seem to moderate, but by the time Exminster was reached, the coachman had determined his horses could not continue to find purchase for their hooves, and pulled into the courtyard of the George. The guard climbed down and wrenched open the door, only to find himself the object of Nurse's baleful stare. "What is the meaning of this?" she demanded.

"Lord bless you, ma'am, we'd slide into a ditch, were we to go on," he retorted, nettled. "Come down now and go inside."

This speech did little to mollify Nurse. "We must reach Exeter by this evening," she explained sharply.

"Well, you might be able to hire a chaise. There won't be no stages running, not in this weather, there won't. Are you coming down or not?"

Nurse made no further attempt to demur, and in a few minutes had gathered up their bandboxes and was shepherding Natia toward the door of the inn. Both were too much occupied to heed the sound of approaching hoofbeats until a curricle-and-four drew up behind the coach and a wrathful voice demanded to know what cow-handed ensign-bearer had blocked the passage before the door.

"Devon!" Natia gasped under her breath, before hurrying inside, the tears starting to her eyes. "Do you think he saw us, Nettle?"

It would appear that he hadn't, for he commanded the groom seated beside him to go to the horses' heads, and himself jumped down from the curricle. "You!" he said, advancing on the coachman. "Have you had for passengers a lady accompanied by her abigail?"

The coachman recollected that he had had three female passengers, but none that fitted any description of the Quality. "Best ask inside," he concluded.

"Though I doubt any other coach has made it this far."

Fortunately for Natia, Devon concluded he had somehow lost the trail. Returning to the curricle, he turned his horses and set off back along the way he had come to pick it up again. Natia, peeping from a window blind, heaved a sigh of heartfelt relief. "I am a wretch to have drawn you into this, but I never dreamed he would follow us," she told Nurse in a worried tone. "However do you suppose he knew?"

Nurse permitted herself the luxury of letting the question go unanswered. "You run along and bespeak a pot of tea while I search out a chaise to hire. If we don't reach Exeter tonight, there's no way we'll make the boat to Greece tomorrow. Don't forget to use the common room, and pay the bill with small coins."

"You may be sure I see the importance of appearing ordinary. I doubt Devon would recognize me in this gown. I must look a positive dowd."

Nurse, her mind relieved, adjured her to take care and hurried off to hire a conveyance, never dreaming that Natia would order an excellent repast. By the time she returned, the damage was done. The landlord was serving Natia, his demeanor mute testimony to the fact that he had seen through her disguise. Nurse, seeing no help for it, sensibly sat down and made a good meal herself.

The rest of the journey passed without incident. The weather remained inclement, but neither Natia nor Nurse found it daunting. By the time they reached the outskirts of Exeter, the sky had lost some of its laden hue, and the sunset revealed a glow of red where it showed signs of breaking through the clouds. Even so it was nearly dark when the chaise turned in under the archway to the courtyard of the Checquers. The landlord, who met them upon their entrance into the inn, surveyed them in a disinterested manner and made no move to come forward. Nurse thrust herself in front of Natia and demanded a bedchamber for herself and her daughter. Her voice, which had become gruff, brooked no possibility of refusal, but it was the coins she produced from a pocket in her voluminous skirts which impressed their host. In a very little time they found themselves in possession of a small apartment on the top floor under the eaves, overlooking the chicken run at the back of the house. Nurse went around unshuttering the windows to air the room, her remarks on the slatternly habits of the management pungent and to the point; but Natia was too weary to care. Nurse's first concern was to get her into a nightgown, but by the time she had seen her tucked into bed and had gone below to procure a bowl of chicken soup, Natia had fallen fast asleep.

Sounds of wagons rumbling over the cobblestoned streets en route to the quayside floating up to them through the open windows awakened them early the following morning. Nurse went down to the kitchens where, as she had guessed, only one undersized child was dawdling about in stirring up the coals. She brewed a pot of tea, made sandwiches of bread and cheese, and returned upstairs bearing their breakfast on a tray. Soon after they had eaten she was off to the quay, leaving Natia to her own devices, only cautioning her not to venture forth from their room. She had no difficulty in finding the packet that would carry them to Greece, nor in confirming the nine o'clock hour of departure. The return to the inn was necessarily slow, the streets having become congested with every conceivable kind of conveyance, from unwieldly dray-wagons to carts piled high with wooden crates. Not far from the Checquers she suffered the shock of perceiving Lord Devon skillfully maneuvering his team of blood-chestnuts through the crush of traffic and heading her way. In a flash she whisked herself around a corner, and by the time his lordship came abreast of the spot, she had managed to lose herself in the crowd.

Devon had spent a trying morning, preceded by an equally frustrating day. At times it had seemed he had run his quarry to earth, only to find he had lost the trail. He had backtracked several times without success until, upon revisiting the George in Exminster, he had come upon a description of two ladies traveling together who had been set down by a cross-country coach. In the beginning the landlord had taken no particular notice of the daughter. Her frock had been plain, dowdy, in fact. For himself he preferred ladies much given to ruffles and filmy lace. Her hair? He was not sure. Blond, he thought, what he had seen of it escaping from under her bonnet. He was sorry, but his lordship would understand that, except for a certain air of protectiveness about the mother, he had at first seen little of distinction in a pair so modestly dressed. It was only later that he became convinced the younger of the two most certainly must be a lady of quality—down on her luck, as the saying went. No, he could not say whence they had gone. His lordship might inquire at Crossman's Livery just down the street; perhaps, since the stage had ceased to run, the ladies had sought private transport to continue on their journey.

Devon needed no further encouragement; he was gone on the landlord's words, feeling highly elated. The long and short of it was he had been following the wrong scent, never thinking that Natia might be traveling in disguise. He had no difficulty in finding out they had indeed hired a carriage from Crossman, though the intelligence that they were bound for Exeter did give him a shock. No, he thought, they could not be so foolish as to embark upon a voyage to Russia unprotected by a male. He went back to the George presently, bespoke a room, ate his dinner, and retired to bed.

To one with a nagging little worry tugging at the fringes of his consciousness, a sound sleep was almost an impossibility. Devon dozed fitfully, time and again startled awake by a vague uneasiness which he could not identify. Around one o'clock exhaustion took its toll, and he was able at last to fall into a deep slumber which lasted until a sudden commotion created by early morning revelers passing beneath his window rudely jarred him awake. Just enough light seeped in through the window blinds to enable him to read the hands of his fob-watch lying on the bedside table. Five o'clock, he groaned, and sank back down upon the pillows. Unable to compose himself, he gave up all attempt to go to sleep again, and got up.

There was no one in the coffee room when he went downstairs. Disgruntled, he strolled out of doors and to the stables. One brief order, coupled with a coin pressed into his palm, sent an ostler scurrying to summon Devon's groom and to hitch his team to the curricle. Under way at last, they proceeded down the street at a sober pace, but once free of the town Devon dropped his hands and sent the horses thundering along the highway to Exeter at breakneck speed. Beside him Grimsly preserved an unbending silence for several miles. It was then borne in upon the groom that his lordship, having first eschewed breakfast, now seemed bent on breaking the speed record set by Sir Edmund Templeton the previous year. The temptation was great; he longed to clutch the seat. Instead he sat sedately still, seemingly unmoved.

Devon, who until now had been too much occupied in controlling his team to think of much else, slowed the pace and gave himself over to a careful analysis of Natia's flight. From the moment his valet informed him a housemaid had espied her entering a hired hackney with Nurse at the odd hour of six o'clock in the morning, and with numerous bandboxes, matters had been securely in her hands. That she was following a prearranged plan he did not doubt; that she anticipated a satisfactory conclusion prior to being missed seemed a distinct possibility.

The sudden oath which split the silence startled Grimsly into very nearly parting company with the seat. Before he had quite recovered his balance, Devon swore again and set his horses at a dangerous gallop down a hill. Grimsly cast caution to the winds. "If I may say so, my lord, the road does seem a mite treacherous," he ventured in a voice that shook only slightly.

Devon cast him one fleeting look. "Are you instructing me in how to drive?" he said ominously.

The groom subsided, fearful of distracting his lordship's attention, and frankly clung to his seat, relieved to see his lordship's gaze fixed on the road again. The stretch of highway which opened out before them ran straight for several miles, then banked and curved again for the final run to Exeter. They feather-edged a corner without slackening speed, and pressed on. The team was responding gallantly, but by the time it reached the outskirts of Exeter, the horses' flanks were heaving and foam-flecked. Devon checked their headlong pace, then dropped them into a canter and entered town at a smart trot. They were on their way to the quayside when Nurse caught sight of them.

The tang of salt air, and the fetid smell of the waterfront, smote Devon's nostrils some little time before he arrived at the quay. The dock was piled with cargo destined to be loaded on tall, masted ships standing in the open harbor awaiting their turn in line. Dockhands scurried about amid the chaos, egged on by sailors whose language was as colorful as the life they led. One aging strumpet moved among them, the outline of her sagging breasts clearly revealed beneath her flimsy garment. Shrieking urchins at play amid the casks and kegs only added to the din. The whole scene was nauseous with the odor of unwashed bodies and mouldering rubbish.

Devon drew the curricle up beside a sailor who was lounging against the crumbling brick wall of a warehouse with a straw between his teeth. "Would you be so good as to point out the barque *Odyssey*? I understand she is due to sail today."

The seaman removed the straw from his mouth. "'Tain't none sailin' terday, yer honor," he replied, straightening himself respectfully in happy anticipation of a generous gratuity.

Devon looked perplexed. "I have just shortly recalled seeing her listed among the departures reported in yesterday's *Gazette*. Are you certain? She is a merchantman bound for the Mediterranean," he added in way of amplification.

The sailor sagged back against the wall. "I done told ye she ain't," he said. "Mebbe termorrer."

Devon flipped a coin, which was deftly caught, and set his team forward. "Thank God I perused yesterday's paper," he remarked to Grimsly. "They have booked passage on the *Odyssey*. There can be no other explanation."

"If I may say so, my lord, it does seem they mean to sail, what with the bandboxes and all."

His lordship gave a derisive snort. "I mean to scour this town from end to end," he said grimly. "They will be forced to seek lodging for the night. We will find them."

He would soon find his optimism to be misplaced. To the sailor, as to others of his kind, one day was much like another. Instead of its being Tuesday, as he thought, it was Wednesday. While Devon searched the inns and other lodgings, the *Odyssey* was destined to stand out to sea with Natia and Nurse aboard.

The two women had come to the pier by a tortuous

route, peering around corners and hurrying down side streets, past the shops of merchants and the abodes of the poor, circling always toward the smell of the sea, their passing made stealthy by thoughts of being overtaken. Natia trembled under the rude attention of people who stopped to stare, but fear of being apprehended by Devon spurred her on.

Sailors swarmed over the *Odyssey*, making her ready to sail. Fresh fruit and vegetables were being brought aboard, along with the salt pork, dried beans, and sea biscuits that would make up the majority of the seamen's diet. Natia and Nurse paused beside the pier to watch a procession of livestock being herded up the gangplank. From the number of sheep and goats and crates of chickens going aboard, it could be surmised that the officers would dine much better than the crew.

Natia climbed up the gangplank behind Nurse and was helped down from it by a very redfaced young bo'sun who then led them across the deck. Their cabin was discovered at the end of a companionway and down a short flight of three steps. "It's so small!" Natia gasped, stunned.

The bo'sun blushed more furiously still. " 'Tis the Captain's, ma'am," he mumbled, and stumbled backward through the door.

Nurse wasted no time getting them settled in. A brass-bound trunk found beneath a bunk proved adequate for their gowns, while a washbasin attached to the wall provided space for toiletries. Natia sank down upon a chair, outwardly calm, but inwardly quaking. She felt exhausted and not a little apprehensive. It was all so different from her expectations, so cramped and hot and noisy. Drifting in through the the open porthole came the sound of the last hatch being battened down mingled with the voices of swearing sailors. She twisted around in her seat, her gaze roaming over the cabin. "Nettle, do you think we are doing the right thing?" she asked in a somewhat woe-begone voice.

Nurse looked up from smoothing sheets on the bunks. "We'll go topside in a minute, Missy. You will feel better about it after you freshen up."

Natia obediently went to the washstand and poured cool water into the bowl. A vision of her shining tub back at Devon Hall crossed her mind. Releasing a small sigh, she reached for the bar of soap. "Why should the Captain's cabin contain two bunks?" she asked idly. "I should think he could put the space to better use."

Nurse became very still. "There is something I've been meaning to say," she began with a sternness Natia had not heard from her before. "You are not to leave this cabin unless I am with you. I want your word on it, Missy."

Natia gazed at her, confused. "But why?" she asked. "I promise not to fall overboard."

Nurse did not seem able to meet her eyes. "Sailors who are far from home—away from their wives—well, never mind. You just do as I say."

"I know not to interfere with their work, Nettle. Papa was always angry whenever I got in the way of whatever he was doing."

"That's not what I mean, Missy. Men confined by a long voyage could lose their heads and become dan-gerous if they had to endure the sight of a young woman wandering about the ship alone." Nurse paused and studied Natia closely. "Do you understand what I'm saying?" she asked finally.

Natia bit her lip and dropped her eyes. "I—I think so," she murmured softly.

Nurse turned away abruptly and crossed the cabin. "We'd best hurry up on deck if we're to have a last glimpse of England," she said, holding open the door.

In a matter of moments they were leaning on the

rail watching sailors toiling at the oars of long boats towing the *Odyssey* out into the harbor past small craft skimming lightly over the waves and larger ships standing closer in to shore. The sails were spread to catch a strengthening breeze, the anchor splashed free of the water, and the *Odyssey* began to make headway. Natia watched the shoreline recede, her ears filled with orders bellowed from the quarterdeck. She would have liked to understand the meaning of such phrases as taking a reef in the mainsail and easing off the port tacks, but supposed she would soon come to know the language of the sea.

The third day out saw them well into the Mediterranean Sea, and running before the wind with every inch of canvas spread. A low bank of clouds obscured the horizon and dense patches of fog lay before them on their course. Natia stood beside the helmsman, listening to the rigging singing in the wind, her eyes scanning a sea that had turned a muddy gray and was running high. Nearby, Nurse glanced aloft and frowned to see a low-lying layer of mist obscuring the topsails. Coming aft, the Captain joined them on the quarterdeck and saw that Natia's eyes were wide and worried. "Calm your fears, ma'am," he said, casting a weather eye at the horizon. "Rain is brewing in the west, but we will easily outrun it."

Natia wasn't satisfied with this assurance, but she hesitated to display her inexperience before men to whom vagaries in the weather were an everyday occurrence. Later in their cabin her attempts to reveal her thoughts to Nurse met with a repetition of the Captain's words. Still she could not rid herself of the notion that some ominous aura hung over the ship, threatening to destroy them all. Later when they went back to the main deck, they found that the fog had closed in around them. It was an eerie scene. The ship seemed afloat in an impenetrable sea of mist.

Suddenly, from aloft, the lookout cried, "Sail, ahoy. Fore-quarter starboard."

All pandemonium broke loose. Seamen swarmed into the rigging, letting out more sail. Cannon were run out, primed, and loaded. "Helmsman, steady as she goes," the Captain ordered, his feet braced wide apart. "Mr. Rodgers, escort the ladies below."

"Aye, aye, sir," the mate grinned, pleased to have a moment more in Natia's company.

It was rough going, returning to their cabin. The wind grew stronger, sending the ship straining as it fought its way through increasingly choppy seas. Natia stumbled in the companionway and would have fallen but for the mate's hand beneath her elbow. Devon Hall came to her mind, seeming a peaceful haven in retrospect. She shrugged the thought away and smiled upon Mr. Rodgers. Very well, they would lock the door. He was not to worry. It would remain locked until his return.

"Whatever do you suppose is worrying them?" she asked Nurse the moment they were alone.

"Sailors always worry for the safety of their ship," Nurse replied, keeping her own fears to herself.

"What a horrible thought," Natia remarked, crossing to sit down upon her bunk. "Do you think Lord Devon is following us still?"

"Not unless he has grown wings, Missy. There is not another ship due this way for weeks."

"Perhaps he owns a yacht."

"Perhaps," agreed Nurse. "The more I think of it, the more I devoutly hope he does."

A deafening noise split the air, sending Natia flying into Nurse's arms. Within minutes the ship came alive with the din of battle. They huddled together in a corner of the cabin, sounds of the struggle raging over the decks clearly audible. It was a slaughter. The *Odyssey*'s crew, stout seamen all, proved no match for the seasoned raiders who attacked. In a very short time the ring of clashing sword blades outside in the companionway quickly terminated on a bloodcurdling scream, and the door to the cabin flew open under the crash of a booted foot.

"Good God!" Natia gasped, appalled. "Pirates!"

The huge Turk seemed to fill the narrow doorway, his yellowed teeth gleaming in a dark face. "Allah be praised," he breathed, catching sight of Natia. "A pearl beyond price."

Natia stared at him in befuddled amazement. "You speak French!" she exclaimed.

He was upon her in two strides. "You will bring a fortune in Damascus," he grinned, dragging her to her feet.

Struggling to free herself from his grasp, she brought her knee up against his groin with all the force she could summon. The next instant she went crashing to the floor, felled by a vicious blow which left her stunned.

Nurse dropped to her knees beside Natia and raised her in her arms. "Heathen!" she spat at the Turk bent over nearly double with the pain.

Suddenly a second raider was in the room. "What in Allah's name is this, you limb of Satan," he roared at his stricken comrade. "Would you mar the face of such a beauty? Touch her again and you are dead!"

Natia, feeling dizzy and slightly nauseous, turned her head to look at him. He was elegantly garbed in silken robes banded from neck to hem with sable. Around his waist he wore a belt of hammered gold studded with cabochon emeralds of monstrous size. Natia felt numb with shock. Only a slaver could possess such jewels. She would be sold at auction to the highest bidder!

As if reading her thoughts, he shrugged. "You will bring a king's ransom on the block. Until then your every move will be watched. It is useless to attempt escape; my men will be posted outside your door. If

you wish to stroll about the decks, they will see you
do not throw yourself overboard."

Natia summoned up a courage she had not known
she possessed. "My maid: she stays with me," she said
in a remarkably level voice.

The slaver shrugged again and left them, locking
the door behind him.

In the days ahead Natia lost all sense of direction.
From the position of the sun they could be sailing
east, but in her present state she could not be sure of
it. Meals were brought to their cabin at all hours of
the day or night, but since the eunuch serving them
spoke only Turkish, nothing could be learned from
him. They went on deck often to stroll about, osten-
sibly for exercise, but failed to discover the fate of the
Odyssey's crew. Gradually the reality of her own fate
seeped into Natia's numbed brain and became almost
more than she could bear.

CHAPTER FOUR

In Marseilles, on the southeastern coast of France, Lord Devon was stepping ashore from his private yacht. He went immediately to the offices of Trans-World Shipping and asked to see the person in charge. Ushered into the inner sanctum of Adam McVey, he lost no time in coming to the point. "A young female relative of mine is a passenger on a ship of yours, the *Odyssey*," he said. "I will be greatly in your debt if you will furnish me with a list of her ports of call."

Mr. McVey hesitated, choosing his words with care. "It is sometimes difficult to know the exact location of a vessel at any given time, my lord."

Devon smiled encouragement. "Overtaking the *Odyssey* should pose no problem," he explained. "My own *Seahawk* was built for speed."

The agent considered the man before him; his lordship had best be told the truth. "The *Odyssey* is four days late in putting into port, my lord. Turk slavers have lately been reported raiding much farther west than ever before. I'm sorry, my lord, but there have been no storms at sea. The *Odyssey* may well have run afoul of pirates."

Devon's cheeks blanched under their tan. "Where

would they have taken the captives?" he said with a
control the agent had to admire.

"Damascus, I should think. The auction houses there
are famous in the East."

Devon's hands clenched together until the knuckles
showed white. "I know nothing of the ways of slavers,"
he heard his own voice saying. "What course would
you follow if you were in my shoes?"

"Might I inquire if your lordship's relative is come-
ly and—a virgin?" At Devon's nod, he continued, mus-
ing: "She will be taken to a private auction house
where she will bring the highest price. A rescue is
out the question, my lord. You would be torn limb
from limb. I would advise you to dispatch an agent
in an attempt to buy her back. If I may suggest it, I
have the very man for you. He is a Turk, but entirely
trustworthy."

"A Turk!" Devon ejaculated, stunned.

"Riafat's history may interest you, my lord. It seems
that at the time the old Sultan fell ill of a seizure and
died, his father held the post of tutor in the household of one of the innumerable royal princes. Riafat
swears he had nothing to do with the plot to put young
Rahib on the throne in his brother's stead, but retribu-
tion in the East can be swift and horrible at times. On
the new Sultan's orders, all members of Rahib's household were sewn into weighted sacks and thrown alive
into the Bosporus. Riafat escaped a like fate only because he chanced to be from home when the massacre
took place."

Devon sat still as a statue, not because he was unmoved by the story, but because the certainty that
Natia's very nature would lead her into unspeakable danger rose up to haunt him. Holding his panic
at bay, he said, "It is a difficult task I have set myself,
McVey. The least leak in my plans and I could end
up in the Bosporus."

"The victims were denied the mercy of strangulation, my lord. Even now, thoughts of what they must have suffered become almost more than Riafat can stand. His sister, whom he dearly loved, was only twelve years old at the time. His hatred runs deep, my lord."

"If you are certain he will not fail me—"

"He will serve you faithfully, for vengeance, if for no other reason. French is usually employed by the slavers, but Turkish is the language of the streets. I presume you do not speak it, my lord. Should you find it necessary to enter Turkey yourself, I doubt you would come out alive without Riafat."

McVey's confidence in the Turk was substantiated when, two weeks later, he went hand over hand up a rope dangling over the leeward side of the *Seahawk* and jumped lightly onto the deck. She was riding at anchor close in to shore, hidden under the boughs of trees spreading a blanket of protection out over the water from the banks of the river Barada. Riafat had memorized the location of every hatch and coil of rope until he knew the deck of the ship like the back of his hand. Surefooted, he moved as silently as a wraith past watchful crewmen straining their ears for the least indefinable sound, slipped through the door into Lord Devon's cabin, and flung himself on his face at his lordship's feet.

Devon reached down and lifted him up. "We will have no more of this," he said, embarrassed. "You are not my slave, you great fool."

"My size is not uncommon among my people, lordship. It will serve to draw attention to my face, leaving yours to go unnoticed. I bring bad news, lordship. The old one will be sold in the open market place in the morning. Does your lordship wish to purchase her? She should bring only a few dinars, lordship."

"Could you manage it without betraying our presence here?"

Riafat grinned. "Who would question a poor farmer seeking solace for his lonely bed, lordship? Allah be praised, it will go well."

"And the other one—Lady Devon?"

"Lordship, there is no chance. She goes to the harem of the Sultan. The slaver is a wily man, lordship. He brought her to the attention of the agha kislar. There is another one your lordship may wish to buy. I was told her hair is golden as the sun, and her skin silken to the touch. Her price may exceed twenty thousand gold dinars, lordship."

"I really cannot endure it, Riafat."

"Perhaps a maiden from Cathay, my lord?"

"You really must cease 'lordshipping' me with every other breath. You will henceforth name me—Rezza, I believe. Yes, that will do nicely. I shouldn't wish you inadvertently honoring me with my title on the streets of Constantinople. Yes, Riafat. You read me correctly. We will secure her ladyship's freedom before the gates of Topkapi Palace close behind her. "

"If Allah wills it—Rezza. May your fondest dream bear fruit."

"You have a quaint way of putting it, but you couldn't be more apt. We will need a carefully thought-out plan if we aren't to end up skewered on some Janissary's pike. Be a good fellow and draw a map of the city."

Riafat sat down at a table and drew forward a sheet of paper. "As you see, the waters of the Dardanelles make their way into the Sea of Marmara," he explained, beginning to sketch. "And just here, atop a high hill, Topkapi Palace overlooks the city from the west side of the Bosporus, between the Sea of Marmara and the place where the Golden Horn joins the Bosporus. It is surrounded by a high stone wall, Rezza, and well guarded."

"What is the approach to the palace?"

"A narrow street winds upward from a landing pier

on the Golden Horn. The climb is steep, with homes and shops crowded together along the way, but it is one of the more heavily traveled streets in the city. Two important mosques and the Grand Bazaar are located not far from the Palace."

"It couldn't be better," Devon remarked. "We will lose ourselves in the throngs of the faithful on their way home from prayer."

Riafat counted thirty-two summers, but in all his years he had never met the equal of his lordship. Suddenly he was frightened. "We would need an army," he ventured, eyes carefully on the sketch before him.

Devon chuckled. "We have an army: you, myself, and my valet. Marston is a man of many talents; his own mother would not recognize him in disguise. You look worried, Riafat. You needn't be, you know. At home we call it diversionary tactics. It's quite simple, really. We secrete ourselves in some likely doorway and wait for the conveyance transporting her ladyship to the Palace to come abreast. A disturbance of some sort will draw the attention of the guards and afford us an opportunity to remove her from under their noses."

"A disturbance, lordship?"

"You have hit upon the nub of our problem, Riafat. Would you by any chance have friends eager for a bit of sport?"

"The Sultan's eunuchs will be escorting her ladyship. The Janissaries have always despised them, calling them half-men. They would enjoy an opportunity to bait them; no one else would dare. They need only think it is baiting."

"Marston will need a small boat to wait for us at some fortunate spot. I'm sorry the arrangements are left up to you, but I dare not venture into the city before I must."

"I will always carry with me the horror of the Sultan's unspeakable cruelty to my family, lordship.

This vengeance I take may be small, but it is all that is possible. I am content."

"The *Seahawk* will return for you and Mrs. Nettle tomorrow after dark. Be wary of your purchase, my friend. Her tongue can be razor sharp."

"Woman and the she-camel have much in common, lordship. An occasional beating helps."

Whatever means Riafat employed, he was waiting with a much bedraggled and subdued Nurse when the yacht dropped anchor the following night. She had thought she would spend the rest of her life toiling for some filthy heathen, treated little better than an animal and grieving over the fate of Natia. From the moment she sank exhausted onto the deck of the *Seahawk*, until the end of her days, she would remain fiercely loyal to Lord Devon.

Natia had fared much better than Nurse, though she had no way of knowing this at the time. The slaver had allowed them to remain together until the captured *Odyssey* sailed up the Barada to Damascus, but once Damascus was reached, Nurse had been sent to one of the public auction blocks in the city. Female slaves had come aboard to dress Natia in trousers of a diaphanous fabric caught in tight about the ankles, and a short jacket which barely covered her breasts. To a lady bred from the cradle in the ideas of modesty prevailing in the West, it was a devastating experience. She could only sit on her bunk and attempt to cover as much of her bare torso as the skimpy jacket would permit.

Natia had only the haziest notion of the customs and morals of the Turks. She knew vaguely they worshiped a god they called Allah, and that their religion permitted a man several wives and as many concubines as he could afford. But until the Sultan's agent walked into her cabin, she had no conception of the lowly place women occupied in Turkish society.

Natia glanced at him and quickly looked away. She

had never seen a eunuch before, and so could not know that castrated men tend toward flabby bodies and sagging breasts. He was extremely obese, his shaven skull adding to an illusion of great height. He was, in a word, obscene.

"Tell her to stand," he said to the slaver in a tongue strange to Natia's ears.

The slaver obeyed, speaking in French. "You are honored. The agha kislar to our Great Sultan deigns to look at you. On your feet, woman!"

Natia had much to learn. "Go away!" she snapped, hugging her arms more tightly across her breasts.

The slaver turned deathly white and dropped to his knees before the agha. "Mercy, oh great one. Mercy, I beg you," he cried frantically, kissing the hem of the agent's gown. "I couldn't know. She is newly taken, and untrained."

The agha's contemptuous gaze rested on the slaver a moment before he waved him to his feet with a slight movement of one hand. Natia watched the passage, round-eyed, the power the Sultan wielded over his subjects forcibly brought home to her. Slowly she rose and stood trembling under the agha's penetrating stare.

"She is virgin?" he asked the slaver.

"My women examined her, my lord," the slaver replied in a trembling voice. "She has never lain with a man."

"Remove her garments."

Natia was too frightened to resist. The slaver pulled the jacket from her arms and slid the trousers down over her hips until they lay in a heap at her feet. Two pairs of eyes devoured her nakedness, the eunuch's uninterested in the way of a man with a woman, the slaver's with lust. The agha walked slowly around her, his eyes examining every inch of her body. "Her skin is unmarred," he remarked, coming to a halt before her. Taking her breasts in his hands, he kneaded them gently. "They are firm and well rounded," he said. "The Sultan will be pleased. What are you asking for her?"

"Twenty-five thousand gold dinars, my lord."

"I will pay you twenty. Have her aboard my yacht before nightfall."

Natia stood as if turned to stone, her mind incapable of registering the shame. It was as if she were divorced from the scene, as if some other girl stood in her place. The sound of the closing door brought her out of the trance. She was alone, so blessedly alone. Quickly she pulled up the trousers, put on the jacket, and collapsed in a sobbing heap upon the bunk.

One week later she stood by the porthole of her cabin when the agha's yacht reached Constantinople. Despite her misery she could not help being fascinated by the slender minarets towering above the city. Everywhere she looked the golden domes of mosques glittered in the sunlight. There must be hundreds of them, she thought, awed. The throngs of common people crowding the streets on foot mingled with noble lords mounted on horseback and heavily veiled ladies in litters carried by slaves. Natia gazed at the strangeness of it all, intrigued in spite of herself.

Shortly after the yacht tied up at its pier, a eunuch came to fetch her. Swathed in a robe that hid her body completely from view, and veiled so heavily only her eyes were visible, she was hustled ashore and into a litter carried on the shoulders of four black eunuchs. They set off up a narrow street, preceded by the agha kislar. The mere sight of the Sultan's favorite was enough to clear a path through the crowds. Natia could tell from the tilt of her seat that the way was steep, but since the litter was hung with curtains on all four sides, she was enclosed in a cocoon and could not see out. The sound of horses' hooves and raucous laughter was followed almost immediately by the litter being jostled about and forced sideways against a

wall. Natia stared wide-eyed at the curtain hanging
within inches of her nose. The temptation was great.
She longed to lift the flap to peer out, but instinct
stayed her hand. Jeered at and taunted by the Janissaries, the eunuchs soon joined the fray. Natia strained
her ears, but fortunately the insults hurled back and
forth were spoken in Turkish. Suddenly the litter was
on the pavement, momentarily abandoned by the
outraged bearers.

Before she could even gasp, the curtains on the side
of the litter next to the wall parted, and a hand
clamped over her mouth. In a trice she was lifted
out, a stone approximating her weight placed on the
floor of the litter, and the curtains dropped back in
place. Smothered in enveloping robes, held immobile
in a pair of strong arms, she was whisked up a staircase to the flat roof of a building and laid down
stretched out upon her stomach. "Quiet," a voice
hissed in her ear. "Our lives depend upon it." Natia
twitched and tried to turn her head. "Yes, it is I,".
Devon's voice murmured low. "Lie still!"

Down below, the babble grew louder. People came
running from all directions, eager for excitement;
within minutes a pushing, milling throng crowded
the street. Suddenly the agha kislar regained his senses.
Trembling under his fierce glare, the populace shrank
back, and the tiny procession resumed its progress up
the hill. Riafat waited until the laughing Janissaries
moved on down the hill before raising his head to
peer through an opening in the roof. The litter was on
the point of vanishing around a sharp bend in the
street. Grinning, he opened the sack at his feet. I
should be mortified, Natia thought vaguely as they
stripped her naked and clothed her in shapeless
peasant garb. But somehow this time it was different.
"You must walk three steps behind us," Devon instructed while removing her upturned slippers. "Keep
your head down and do not speak, no matter what!"

"Her feet!" Riafat suddenly ejaculated softly.

Devon stared at their tender softness, thinking fast. He scooped up dust from the roof and held it cupped in his hands. "Spit," he said, grinning.

They smeared the mud on her feet and hands, and even on her face. One veil extended from the bridge of her nose to her waist, while another hung down to her eyebrows. Satisfied, Devon stuffed her discarded clothing into the sack and thrust it into her arms. "We must be some distance away before the litter arrives at the Palace gates," he murmured, rushing her down the stairs. "For God's sake, Natia, don't stumble."

She trailed behind them, her eyes riveted to Devon's heels. Each step became an agonizing pain as she shuffled along hunched over as if permanently bowed from toil. The soles of her feet felt on fire, but there was no way to avoid treading on loose stones: the street was strewn with them. She had learned much since her capture; she gritted her teeth and trudged on. At the foot of the hill Devon turned right along the shores of the Golden Horn. Natia was by now in excruciating pain; just when she thought she could bear no more, Devon stopped beside a dhow. The lantern-rigged vessel with its long overhand forward and high poop was an interesting sight, but Natia was too exhausted to appreciate it. "We will enter first, Natia. You must scramble aboard without assistance," he said softly without turning his head.

Somehow she managed it and made her way to the prow of the boat around a strange Turk seated at the tiller. There she sank down upon the deck and let her mind go blank. Only the creaking of the sail disturbed her rest as Devon sat down beside her, his eyes anxiously scanning the shore for the first sign of pursuit.

Dusk had fallen when he touched her arm, startling her awake. They were anchored in a shallow creek, camouflaged from sight by boughs cut from trees and draped about the boat. "I don't know how to thank you," she murmured, sitting up. "I thought sure all was lost."

"Nonsense," he replied in rallying tones. "You have no cause to thank me. Of course I came after you. You are my wife."

"I haven't acted much as if I am," she admitted. "I refused to trust you, when all you have ever done is to treat me with courtesy."

"Ever?" he chuckled, his eyes alight with laughter.

"Well, almost ever. Though I didn't know it when we first met, you had a perfect right to—to kiss me."

"That is very true. I might add I have been wanting ever since to do it again."

"Oh!" she said, foolishly. "Well, I am grateful to you for rescuing me. I don't scruple in telling you I was never so glad to see anyone in my life!"

"By that time you would have been glad to see the devil himself."

"No, you are wrong there. I had already seen him; I shall need to think of some way to express my gratitude."

"It is not your gratitude I want," he replied, lifting her to her feet. "Supper will be cold, I'm afraid. We dare not show a light."

Pain shot up her legs the moment her feet bore her weight. She groaned; she could not help it. Devon scowled and dropped down on one knee before her. "God!" he breathed, gazing in horror at her broken and bloody soles. Picking her up, he carried her to the seat beside the tiller. "Bring water and clean cloths," he said to the Turk she had noticed earlier when she came aboard.

Devon was gentle, but still the tears were rolling down her cheeks by the time the last dressing was bound securely in place.

"This may help, my lady," a voice spoke at her elbow.

Natia accepted the glass of wine, turning startled eyes upon her benefactor, the spurious Turk of the tiller. "Surely it is not the very proper Marston," she said mischievously.

The valet bowed. "If I may say so, my lady, none of us appear quite as we ought."

Devon chuckled. "Let that be a lesson to you, my dear. Depend upon it, Marston is seldom at a loss."

"Listen!" Riafat said sharply, and threw up a hand.

Back on the banks of the Golden Horn, just opposite the entrance to the stream, they heard horses and the creak of leather saddles. With one accord they froze. For ten minutes after the sound of pounding hoofbeats had faded away in the distance, no one moved.

"Allah be praised, they missed us in the dark," Riafat said then. "They will return, lordship."

"Do you think they suspect we came this way?"

"No, lordship. Tonight they merely search. Tomorrow they become desperate."

"Won't they see us in the boat?" Natia asked.

"That," said Devon, "is the very root of the matter."

"I do not wish to appear impertinent, lordship," Riafat began, "but the farm of a cousin lies some forty kilometers to the east. One may be mistaken, but there is a saying that to follow the track of the camel is to become lost in a sea of sand."

Devon digested this. "You amaze me, Riafat," he remarked, intrigued. "Of course we will go to your cousin's farm. I imagine crossing the desert is infinitely preferable to the tender mercies of the Sultan."

Natia's eyes widened. "You mean we are going to walk?" she demanded. "Why?"

"Because the Sultan's troops had the good sense to

look for us outside the city. It was not expected. The Grand Turk is in all probability breathing fire."

"You cannot know what you are saying. He has not even seen me."

"My dear, if I told you he values women somewhat less than magnificent horses, you would be offended."

"I see. We had the audacity to defy him. No doubt he feels insulted."

"No doubt he does. Lopping off heads has become a habit with him. Can you swim?"

"You have all my admiration, Colin, but we are a long way from the sea. I'd rather walk."

"That may be, but I doubt I can part the waters for you. We must take this boat out into the deepest waters of the Horn and sink it to hide it. Be a good girl and contrive to swim ashore here, where the distance is not so great."

"Since there's no help for it, I will. But you must all turn your backs."

She was not quite sure she could swim with her clothing held above the water with one hand, but she intended to try. There would be time enough to let Colin assist her if she found she could not make it. He had seen her naked once; a second time was the very thing she wished to avoid. The shore seemed far away when she eased herself into the water, but she accomplished it willy-nilly and scrambled up the bank to dress.

The men each made the trip twice, bringing with them the sack containing the clothing Natia had been wearing when rescued and the supplies Marston had stowed away in the boat. In case the craft was later discovered at the bottom of the Golden Horn, there would be no positive way to connect her with the fugitives.

No plan for going cross-country had been devised;

they had not foreseen the need of it. After a hurried conference they were of one accord: they would travel by night, guided by the stars, and hide themselves during the daylight hours. Devon watched Riafat empty the wine jugs and refill them with water, and felt suddenly very helpless.

Natia wondered later how she had ever managed to endure the rest of that horrible night. The landscape seemed composed entirely of sharp stones and shifting sand. No sooner had her feet become accustomed to one form of torture than they were subjected to another. They paused often to rest. She suspected herself the cause, but could only feel gratitude for being female. She stumbled and became aware Devon was staring at her. Evidently feeling she was incapable of negotiating the dry gully revealed in the moonlight, he slung her over his shoulder and so took her across it. She thought she would be set down on the other side, but he strode on. She found nothing incongruous about her head hanging down his back. "Thank you!" she murmured, with real gratitude.

It was coming on dawn when they came upon an abandoned dwelling perched atop a hill unexpectedly jutting up from the desert floor. It was a hut actually, built of mud held together with bits of straw. Openings had been left to serve the purpose of a door and windows, but they had never known a covering of any sort. In a less harsh setting the structure would have melted away long before, but in the arid climate of the desert even much of the thatched roof remained. Devon carried Natia inside and lowered her to the dirt floor.

"You will be comfortable enough, I trust," he said. "Wait here. We won't be long."

Curiously enough she wasn't much interested in what they might be planning to do. The air was foul in her nostrils, and she was feeling queasy. Nodding, she stretched out on the floor and tried to take her mind off her stomach.

A little while later the men reentered the hut and ranged themselves along the walls. Marston and Riafat immediately went to sleep, but Devon noted Natia's pallor and became concerned. "I know it is a rude shelter, my dear, but it will shade us from the sun," he offered tentatively.

Natia opened her eyes and shuddered. "It isn't that, Colin. It's just that—I feel so ill. What is causing that odor?"

"I can't do anything about it, Natia. This hut is built on a pile of cow dung for warmth in the winter. Riafat tells me it is a common practice—"

He got no further. Natia gasped, clapped her hand to her mouth, and flew through the door. Embarrassed though she was, Devon's supporting her head with a hand upon her brow while she retched was comforting. He didn't seem to find the experience disconcerting, she thought. Indeed he seemed to know exactly what to do. He wiped her face with a damp cloth and gave her water with which to rinse out her mouth. "Thank you!" she said devoutly.

Some slight sound awakened her in late afternoon. She lay for a moment with her eyes still closed until, her memory flooding back, she sat up with a start. Devon was standing looking down at her. "Awake, are you?" he said. "Good. It is almost time to leave."

"I don't think I can walk another step," she told him candidly. "My feet don't seem to belong to the rest of me."

"You must," he replied, reaching down to pull her up. "Riafat assures me we should reach his cousin's house by daybreak."

She had a very fair notion of what her appearance must be, but she saw nothing for it but to cross to the door in his wake. Feeling somewhat weak, she swayed slightly and was grateful to take his arm. He waited until they were well away from the area to say, "We will stop to eat shortly. You will do better for some food."

She shuddered. "Please," she begged. "If you have any humanity at all, you won't speak to me of food."

Around ten kilometers farther on they came upon a village clearly visible in the moonlight. The houses were constructed of adobe, each with its surrounding wall, clustered about its hub, a deep well.

"The people sleep, lordship," Riafat remarked, studying the village with keen eyes. "The water jugs grow light. I will refill them at the well."

"Are you sure it is safe?" Devon said doubtfully.

"It is as Allah wills, lordship," came Riafat's inevitable reply.

"With your permission, my lord, I will accompany him, in case of trouble," Marston suggested.

Devon nodded and told Natia to cup her hands. "At least you will be able to rinse them off," he said, tipping the last trickle of water into her palms and then handing the now empty jug to Riafat.

Feeling somewhat refreshed, Natia sank to the ground, thankful to rest her feet. Devon sat down beside her and pulled her against his shoulder. "I wonder you didn't leave me to my fate," she said, incurably truthful. "I have behaved abominably."

His smile flashed. "Don't tell me the shoe is on the other foot," he said. "I would hazard a guess you have never before made such an admission."

"No, I don't suppose I have," she confessed. "To own the truth, I imagine I am spoiled."

"Worse and worse," he chuckled. "I suppose the next thing I shall have to face will be your gratitude."

"Why, no," she said sweetly, not to be outdone. "Why should you imagine I know anything of such an emotion?"

"I know nothing of your emotions, my dear, but I should have no difficulty in discovering them."

"Now, that would never do," she replied, determined to have the final word. "I have an independent spirit, sir. Any attempt on your part to—well, to discover my emotions might cause me to run away again. Surely you wouldn't relish spending the next years chasing after an elusive wife."

A muscle twitched at the corner of his mouth. "You wouldn't remain elusive for long, my dear. I've a notion you aren't as straight-laced as you would have me think."

"Not at all," she said. "It is only that after having had a taste of your ideas of propriety towards a lady, you cannot expect me to fall into your arms."

His eyes were alight with laughter. "My what?" he said.

She turned her head to regard him with a challenging eye. "Your appalling ideas of propriety, sir," she said.

His arm tightened about her shoulders. "I think you will find my ideas differ little from those of any husband," she heard him say before his mouth swooped down on hers.

"Well!" she gasped, the moment she was able. "You haven't changed one whit!"

"Not one whit," he agreed, kissing her again. "Lord! What a muddle we have made of it! Here we are out in the middle of God knows where, and there is nothing we can do about it. You should not have fled from me, my dearest. Did you hate me so very much? I had hoped that when you got to know me—when I'd had an opportunity to woo you—Natia, look at me!"

Slowly her eyes met his. "You won't, I know, pretend that you are in love with me. I have gotten us into a mess that may cost us our lives; you aren't obliged to make me feel better about it."

"Don't waste our precious time in arguing, Natia. I am not pretending. I do love you. If we come out of this alive, I swear to you on my honor I won't touch you unless you want it. But we may not come out of it, my dearest. A few kisses may be all we will ever have."

His arms had tightened about her so fiercely while he spoke that the breath was almost crushed out of her. His lips were gentle on hers at first, and then he was kissing her passionately, hungrily, drawing a response from her. She yielded, carried along on the tide of his passion, and found herself returning his kisses with a fervor to match his own.

Riafat and Marston, returning from the village, grinned to see her ladyship locked in his lordship's embrace, being ruthlessly kissed.

"Allah be praised!" murmured Riafat.

"Thank God!" echoed Marston.

"Colin!" Natia begged. "They will see us!"

"Let them!" said his lordship.

CHAPTER FIVE

"It is strange, lordship," Riafat observed, staring at the farm in the early morning light. "My cousin should be up and about by now."

Devon nodded. "We will take no chances," he said. "Wait here, Natia. We shan't be long."

Fear gripped her. "What are you going to do?" she said, groping for his hand.

"Circle around behind the house and come upon it from the back. Don't worry, my dear. Riafat's cousin is no doubt still abed."

Natia hesitated to add to his troubles and obligingly sat down to wait. She did not mind being alone so much until they were around behind the building, out of sight. Then she felt a little shaken. They seemed to be taking a long time about it, she thought, noting the brightening sky. Intent upon the scene before her, she failed to notice a stealthy form creeping up behind her.

He was incredibly ugly and moved with a crablike motion, his hip having been broken as a child and poorly set. The stench of his unwashed body reached Natia's nostrils at the same time his talonlike fingers seized her arm. She looked wildly around, a piercing scream bursting from her throat. She tried to jerk free, but he dealt a smashing blow to her head and half-dragged her along the ground.

Devon erupted from the farmhouse door, yelling like a banshee, with Riafat close behind him. The Turk cast once glance over his shoulder and took to his heels, leaving Natia lying unconscious in the dirt. Devon reached her first and dropped to a knee beside her, in agony until he saw she breathed. Riafat paused and drew back his arm, a knife in his hand. The arm shot forward, the blade flashed in the sunlight, and the Turk pitched forward on his face, the knife buried in his back up to the hilt.

"She lives, lordship?" he said then.

"I think she has a concussion. Save yourself, my friend. He will turn us in. I imagine there is a reward."

"Allah be praised, there will be no reward, lordship. I will bury him in the barnyard under the dung. He will have followed us from the village, lordship. He will not be found to bring trouble to my cousin."

Devon looked up in surprise and followed the direction of Riafat's eyes. "It seems a fitting resting place," he said, rising to lift Natia in his arms and gently kiss her lips.

The house was small, having two rooms, one with a table and chair and a fireplace for cooking, the other with a pallet in one corner. Devon laid Natia down upon the pallet and wondered aloud what else to do.

"Her ladyship is young and healthy. Keep her warm, and nature will do the rest," Marston advised, and went outside with Riafat to bury the Turk.

Devon pulled the shapeless garment from her body and looked around for a quilt. Not finding one, he went into the other room, returning with his robe in one hand and the chair in the other. He stood by the bed a moment, his gaze devouring the sweet sight before him; sighing, he spread the robe over her and sat down to wait, his eyes never wavering from her face.

When did I first love her? he wondered, and could find no answer to his question. He had found pleasure in the arms of many women, but none had touched his soul. How, then, had this one, whom he had scarcely even kissed, managed to do so without trying, when others had tried and failed? Again he could find no answer. She was just there, in his heart and soul, forever.

Marston came hurrying in sometime later to report riders approaching at a gallop from the south. Riafat, desert-bred and wise in the cunning of the nomad before his father turned to teaching, had several times put his ear to the ground. "He judges we have fifteen minutes, my lord. In case he fails to send them on their way, he sent you this," he added, holding out Riafat's knife. "Her ladyship must not be taken alive, my lord."

Devon gazed at Marston with stricken eyes. "I couldn't, old friend. My hand would falter. You must do it for me."

"If I may say so, my lord, I think I knew of your regard for her ladyship before you knew yourself. With your lordship's permission, I will dispatch you both before I turn the knife on myself."

"You have my permission," Devon replied gravely. "We have been a long time together, Marston. God willing, you will live to bounce my sons on your knee one day."

"I trust so, my lord," Marston bowed. What he did not relate was Riafat's graphic description of the Sultan's brutality when it came to matters of the harem. For lesser crimes against the throne than theirs, men had thought themselves fortunate to be drawn and quartered.

Riafat was presumably busy raking dung when the soldiers rode up and halted their horses a discreet distance away from him. He immediately flung himself down before them, his nose touching the ground. The performance that followed amazed Devon and Marston, who were watching from back out of sight at the window. Riafat groveled on all fours, punctuating his replies to their questions with much shaking of his head and banging of his nose in the dung. Finally the Captain of the Sultan's guard spat in his general direction and rode off at a gallop, his troop falling in behind him. They were long out of sight before Riafat rose to his feet. Had not Marston previously mentioned it, Devon would never have realized his ear had been to the ground.

They handed him a cloth soaked in water the instant he crossed the threshold. "The offal ride north, lordship," he said, vigorously scouring his face. "May their wives mate with the jackal, and their sons lie down with whores."

Devon's delighted chuckle filled the room. "I have come to love you as a brother," he said, clapping Riafat on the shoulder. "When I return to England, I hope you go with me. Are you married?"

"No, lordship," Riafat replied, looking startled. "I am a poor man, and the bride-price is high."

"Then there is a girl?"

A dreamy look came upon Riafat's face. "Her skin has the blush of a ripening peach, and her hair is black as the raven's wing. But she is not for me, lordship," he added, sighing. "Allah has not willed it."

"Perhaps he has, Riafat. I will pay the bride-price for you. It is the least I can do. If you do decide to stay with me, you must understand that English law will limit you to one wife."

"The one will do for me. As to your England, lordship, it will be up to her to say."

"Then we will await her decision. But first we must make our way to the Seahawk—how, I have no idea."

"Soldiers are a stupid lot; they loose their tongues at times. It is now safe to the south, lordship."

"Go with Riafat to the ship, Marston," Devon said, turning to his valet. "See what you can do about sending a conveyance of some sort to transport her ladyship. She won't be up to walking."

"If the soldiers should return—"

"They won't. We will stay in the house out of sight, and we've food and water to last for days. Off with you, now. We are wasting time."

Natia's skin looked flushed when Devon returned to her bedside. Frowning, he placed his fingers on her forehead and found it hot. She opened her eyes at the touch, mumbled a few words he could not catch, and closed her eyes again. Devon nearly whooped with joy. It wasn't the blow to her head after all. More probably it was exhaustion.

For the next hour he applied damp cloths to her forehead, wringing them out in cool water and re-placing each with a fresh one the moment it grew warm. But still the fever mounted. She fought the water he tipped down her throat, but he persevered until she swallowed. When she began to thrash about and mutter in delirium, he tossed aside the robe cov-ering her and sponged her body until his shoulders ached. Finally the fever began to abate, and her skin grew cool beneath his hands. Sighing, he drew the robe over her and sank down upon the chair, exhausted.

He must have dozed; the sound of her shuddering awakened him. She was shivering in the grip of a chill, her teeth chattering uncontrollably. In a trice he had stripped off his clothing and was under the cover beside her, her body cradled within his arms, his legs wrapped around her legs, warming her with his warmth. Gradually the shivering ceased and she fell into a peaceful sleep, held snug in his embrace.

She partially woke once in the night and lay half

dozing, dreamily thinking of him and feeling strangely secure, but in the middle of some thought which
became oddly tangled, she drifted to sleep again.

The sun was high when she awoke and lay for a
moment with her eyes still closed. Gradually she became aware that an arm encircled her waist and a
large hand cupped a breast. She gasped and sat up-
right, her eyes wide with shock. Devon! Cool air
touching her chest drew her attention back to herself. Blushing furiously, she flopped back down, the
robe clutched to her chin.

Devon raised up on an elbow and smiled down at
her. "Feeling better?" he said.

"W-what are y-you d-doing here?" she stammered
in a quavering tone.

"Warming you," he replied calmly. "You had a
chill."

"A chill?" she repeated numbly.

"After you had a fever. And were delirious," he
added. "I couldn't understand a word."

"You couldn't?" she blurted, feeling foolish, and
desperately searching her mind for something sensible
to say. "Where are my clothes?"

"On the floor in a wad, I'm afraid. I didn't have
time to fold them neatly."

"You—undressed me?" she whispered, wishing she
could stop muttering inane phrases.

He bent forward and kissed the tip of her nose.
"You don't think I would let another man do so, I
hope," he grinned. "That is a husband's privilege,
sweet."

"It is?" she said stupidly.

His hand closed over hers clutching the robe beneath her chin. "You have no reason to be shy, my
dear. Your body is so very beautiful. Have you no
idea just how lovely you are?"

"Don't, Colin. Please. You can't know—I couldn't
bear—"

He became very still, his eyes bleak. "I love you, Natia. Whatever—happened—it doesn't matter. You must believe that, my dearest. It doesn't matter! I love you!"

"Nothing happened—at least not what you m-mean," she gasped. On seeing the glory leap into his eyes, she burst out weeping. "Oh, Colin!" she wailed, and cried the harder.

"Shh," he soothed, holding her tenderly, comforting her until she calmed. "It can't be as bad as that. Tell me about it."

"I can't," she gulped. "It's too awful."

"It won't seem so terrible after you talk about it. Nothing ever does. Start at the beginning."

She fixed her gaze on the wall opposite and took a deep breath. "The—female slaves—dressed me in—well, you saw what they put on me."

"You looked charming," he encouraged. "Go on."

"That man—the fat one—Colin, I can't!"

"Yes, you can. The fat man: what did he do?"

Natia swallowed the lump in her throat. "He told the slaver to undress me. They—they—"

"They looked at you," he finished calmly, his tone masking the murder in his heart. "There is nothing so bad in that. Then what?"

"The fat one, he—touched—put his hands on—on my breasts. He felt—felt them. Oh, God!"

A muscle twitched in his cheek. "Is that all?" he said levelly.

She nodded, unable to look at him.

"Then we are fortunate," he told her flatly. "It will be a simple thing to lay your ghosts. Do you trust me, Natia?"

She looked at him, puzzled. "Of course I do," she said.

His hand again closed over hers clutching the robe to her chin. At his first move to lower the cover, she resisted, shaking her head. "He—touched me," she breathed, the horror of the remembrance staring from her eyes.

"My touch will erase the memory of his, my love. I mean to do a very thorough job of it. Now will you let me bare you?"

She found she didn't mind so much after all. Flushing slightly, she allowed him to lower the robe to her waist. He kissed her gently and then raised his head to gaze upon her breasts. "You are so beautiful," he murmured, lightly touching her breasts. Natia shivered, but he persisted, stroking slowly over and over them until her trembling ceased.

"Now, that wasn't so bad, was it?" he said.

A smile trembled on her lips, and with a queer little sound between a sigh and a groan, she drew his head down to the pink-tipped mounds. Smiling to himself, he gathered her breasts in bold hands and buried his face in them, trailing kisses over the soft flesh until she quivered with pleasure and thrust her fingers through his hair.

The sight and feel of her roused his passions terribly, but he forced himself to reach for the robe and cover her. "Until I sat in an office in Marseilles and learned you could be lost to me forever, I never knew how much I loved you, Natia. I want you, and I think you want me. But I won't take you in this place. I want it to be beautiful for you, my darling. I will wait until we are aboard the *Seahawk*."

She lowered her eyes, and for a few moments he gazed at the lashes trembling against her cheeks. Then he bent and pressed his lips to hers. "I must know, Natia," he said softly. "Do you love me?"

She nodded, a tremulous smile curving her lips, and buried her face in his throat.

"When did you know?" he asked, holding her close.

"When I was sick, and you held my head."

He gave a sudden shout of laughter. "Good God,

could it not have been when you thrilled to my kisses the day we met?"

Her head shot up. "Your conduct was deplorable and you know it!" she said. "The very idea! Kissing a stranger—"

"Don't forget the breeches," he teased.

"Say what you will, you thought you had come across a—"

"A convenient tumble in the hay? You can't blame me for that. How the deuce was I to know?"

"Well, you should have known," she declared. "You can't have spent all your life with the muslin set."

His lips twitched. "I hadn't taken a vow of celibacy," he said.

Mischief gleamed in the eyes twinkling up at him. "I own I wondered about it at the time," she admitted, "but after all, you know, I could always have bitten you."

"What a bungling incompetent you must think me," he replied, grinning. "You wouldn't have stood a chance. I wasn't a monk then, nor am I one now. Before you get more than you are bargaining for, you will do well to dress."

"The thing is, Colin, you are between me and my clothes."

"I have seen you naked before, remember. I spent yesterday afternoon sponging your body to bring the fever down."

"Well, but I was unconscious then."

"You have become used to slaves," he chuckled, bounding from the bed. "I'm not a trained hand-maiden, my dear, but I am willing to learn."

She could not help but look at him. His body was lean and well-proportioned, with broad shoulders and muscular thighs, and his skin was smooth and tanned. He straightened from picking up her clothing and turned to face her, the remark he was about to make dying stillborn on his tongue. Eyes round, she stared, unable to tear her gaze away until, suddenly embarrassed, she hid her face in her hands.

He was beside her on the instant. "Sweetheart, sweetheart," he murmured, taking her hands in his. "You mustn't be frightened. It is only that my body is made for loving yours. I thought you understood."

"I wasn't frightened," she admitted. "It was just that—"

"You have never seen a naked man before. That is as it should be, dearest. I will teach you all you need to know. And now, if you will look the other way, I will dress. Join me when you're ready. Do hurry," he added after she obediently turned her head. "I don't know about you, but I'm hungry."

There was little she could do to tidy herself for the day. She smoothed her hair as best she could with her hands, and did it up again. Grimacing, she shook out the skirts of the shapeless gown and went into the other room.

Devon was foraging among their supplies. "How does bread and fruit strike you?" he said, glancing up.

"That will be fine," she replied absently. "Where are Riafat and Marston?"

"Gone to the *Seahawk* for help. Don't worry, sweet. Marston will return in a few days with a cart of some sort for you to ride in."

"Of all the silly starts," she said scornfully. "We should have gone with them."

"There was no question of it, Natia. I thought you had a concussion."

"Well, I didn't. If we leave now, perhaps we could catch up with them."

"Don't be goosish, my dear," he recommended. "Neither of us speaks Turkish. Eat your breakfast."

"Colin, will you listen to me!" she cried, exasperated. "I want to know your plans!"

"God, but I'm proud of you," he countered. "Any

other woman would have succumbed to the vapors long before now. With you by my side, there is nothing I can't do."

"I know what it is," she said. "You have no plan."

"Ah, but I have, my little spitfire. The *Seahawk* will drop anchor in the Barada every night until we go aboard. A few more days should see us on our way to England."

"I can only suppose you have taken leave of your senses. The soldiers—"

"They have left the area, my dear. It does seem shocking, doesn't it? But then, I suppose they have been idling around Constantinople and have forgotten their trade. I am very obliged to him, but the Captain of the troop would do better to cover his flanks. Do sit down, Natia, and put your anxious mind at rest."

She considered it a horrid set-down, but realized she had invited it. "How shall we pass the time?" she began chattily, taking the chair he held for her. "Mama and I played a game you might enjoy. One calls out a list of words, and the other says whatever pops into his head. It can be splendid fun."

He was wrapping a slice of bread about a piece of cheese, but he looked up and said: "I am long past my infancy, sweet."

"Oh?" she said. "Well, perhaps we could play charades. I pantomime some famous saying, and you guess what it is. Would you like that?"

"I would not!"

"That is no answer," she said, holding out her hand for his bread and cheese. "Thank you. Really, Colin, you are being most uncooperative. We can't just sit here for days with nothing to do."

"If you weren't such an innocent, my girl, you would know there is plenty I can do, short of carrying you to that bed."

Suddenly her head turned toward the door. "It is a

pity you will be denied, my lord," she said demurely, jumping to her feet. "Unless I am much mistaken, Marston is coming now. I hear the cart."

He was on her in two strides. "Get down, you little fool," he growled, dragging her to the floor. "It can't be Marston."

"Well! Of all the ways to talk!" she gasped. "I will thank you to get off my back!"

"For once in your life, do as you are told! We are in mortal danger. If we are quiet, whomever it is may pass on by."

When the sound of squeaking wheels turned in toward the house, Devon cautiously raised his head and peered out of the window. A lone peasant sat slumped in the seat of a rickety wagon pulled by a magnificent horse. Devon's brows shot up. Pure Arabian, he judged, grinning. "Calm yourself, my dear," he said. "It is Riafat's cousin."

"Do you think we should show ourselves?" she asked, sitting up. "What if it isn't?"

"The family breeds Arabian horses; I own Arabians myself. But how the devil do I communicate with him?"

"Try French. The slaver spoke it."

The Turk crossed the threshold a few minutes later and stopped dead in his tracks, his eyes fairly starting from his head.

"Bonjour, Monsieur," Devon said, coming forward. "Parlez-vous français?"

"Yes, I speak French," the Turk replied in perfect English. "Perhaps you would be more comfortable in your own tongue?"

Devon was staggered. "You know who we are?" he gasped, stunned.

"Of a certainty, sir," the Turk replied impassively. "Everyone has heard of the missing *gedikli* from the Sultan's harem. Be calm, my friend. I am only surprised to find you here."

"You have a cousin by the name of Riafat?"

"So?" said the Turk. "It is to be expected. I am Ibrahim, third cousin to Riafat. How may I serve you?"

"We are Lord and Lady Devon. My wife was captured by slavers and sold to the Sultan. Riafat helped me to rescue her, but she fell ill. He and my valet are out looking for a conveyance to transport her to my yacht. That is the story in a nutshell."

The Turk's eyes moved from Devon to Natia and back to Devon. "If I may have a word with you in private?" he requested.

"Natia," Devon said, nodding toward the other room. She saw to her dismay that he meant it, and went with lagging step. She thoroughly intended leaving the door ajar, but saw he hadn't taken his eyes off her, and shut it with a snap. "Now," he said, turning back to the Turk.

"Only virgins are purchased for the Sultan's harem," Ibrahim began without preamble. "The agha kislar is much feared, my lord, and with reason. No slaver would lie to him."

"He had no need to lie," Devon replied levelly. "It will sound strange to you, I know, but in my country things are rather different. We are married, Ibrahim. I just haven't consummated it as yet."

The Turk read the truth in his eyes and bowed. "Customs vary, my lord," he said. "Perhaps some of ours make no sense to you."

"If you will agree to assist us, and I devoutly hope you will, you must know you can trust us. I would feel the same."

"Perhaps I will assist you, my lord. Perhaps not. It seems a man from a village a few kilometers from here has disappeared. His wife claims he left in the early hours of last evening to follow strangers seen at the well. Whether she wails for his return, or for the loss of great wealth he promised, only Allah knows."

"He is buried under the dung in your barnyard. He would have revealed our presence here. Riafat had no choice."

"The widow's tale is strange, my lord," Ibrahim said after a thoughtful moment. "It will bring the soldiers down on you. I will take you to my uncle."

"Thank you," Devon said simply. "I am too desperate to turn you down, though I know we shouldn't involve you in our troubles."

"You will find no love for the Sultan in the camp of my uncle, my lord. My father is brother to Sheik Abdullah den Kallaj, as was Riafat's father. If you are friend to Riafat, you are friend to us all. The soldiers would never search a wagonload of dung. You will be safe hidden beneath it."

Devon's eyes widened. "Is there no other way?" he said. "I can manage it, but her ladyship would be bound to become ill."

"Even a drunken Janissary could not fail to identify her, my lord."

"Riafat provided her with veils. Only her eyes would show."

"Then she will ride with me. The trip will last until late afternoon, but cracks in the wagon floor will allow you air."

Ibrahim set off down the dusty track which served as a road at a pace faster than would have been expected. The farm was soon lost to view behind undulating hills, and gradually the fringes of the true desert opened up before them. Natia had expected only sand as far as the eye could see, and so was surprised when they came upon pasture land where sheep and goats were grazing.

Ibrahim drew the wagon to a halt and jumped down to the ground. "Wait here," he said, striding off to converse with the shepherds tending the flocks.

Natia leaned down to make her voice audible to Devon. "It's all right, Colin," she assured him. "Ibrahim is talking to some men."

"Who are they?" his voice came faintly to her ears.

"I don't know, but they seem friendly."

Ibrahim returned to the wagon grinning from ear to ear. "We are in luck," he said, climbing up to the seat. "Men of my uncle's tribe are camped at an oasis a short distance away. They are returning from delivering horses to the stables of the Sultan."

About fifteen minutes after they resumed their journey, the oasis appeared before them as a patch of green in the distance. The horse quickened his pace without urging and in a few minutes had trotted in under the shade of palm trees growing around a pool of water. Ibrahim spoke rapidly in Turkish to tribesmen tending meat roasting over a fire. They looked startled, then grinned and burst into laughter. To Natia's utter astonishment they immediately set about the business of removing the dung from the wagon, their amusement evident in their twinkling dark eyes and smiling lips.

In a matter of moments they had uncovered Devon and were lifting him to his feet. He was white and shaken and would have fallen had not a tribesman supported him with an arm about his shoulders. A rug had been between his body and the dung, but even so Natia knew he must have suffered terribly. He stood swaying and gasping for air; to her intense relief, he recovered rapidly and even managed a quip. "Remind me never to go near the stables," he said. "God! How I would like a bath!"

"There is a small pool in that clump of trees, my lord," Ibrahim answered, pointing to a smaller patch of green a short distance away. "You, Yussef," he added to a tribesman. "Bring soap and clean clothing for our guests. You will find her ladyship's attire in the sack."

"I couldn'tl" Natia gasped. "It—it is—meant for the harem."

"Yussef will loan you his burnous. We are a civilized people, my lady. You will have complete privacy while you bathe."

The pool was fed by a spring bubbling to the surface through a fissure in an outcropping of rock unexpectedly jutting from the landscape. The banks surrounding it were shaded by tall trees and carpeted with moss and fern. The bottom of the pool was smooth, the water cool and clear.

"I don't know about you," Devon remarked, stripping off his shirt, "but modesty won't keep me out of there a moment more than need be."

"I'm too far gone to care," Natia agreed, reaching for the hem of her gown. Pulling it off over her head, she tossed it on the ground and stepped into the water.

Devon paused to enjoy the sight of her rounded bottom before pulling off his trousers and wading in after her. "I'll wash your back if you'll wash mine," he said, swimming up beside her.

She ceased her paddling about, her feet touching the bottom. "You never give up, do you?" she said.

"Don't be foolish," he replied. "We both smell to high heaven. I'll do you first."

Turning her about, he lathered her shoulders and back and washed her smooth skin with his hands. "We would be better with a cloth," he remarked, rinsing her off. Finished, he pushed her head under water.

"Welll" she sputtered, blinking the drops from her eyes. "Of all the—"

"Hold still," he instructed, attacking her hair with the soap. "It can use a good scrubbing." When he had finished, he calmly pushed her under again.

When her head popped out of the water, he had his

back to her. "Now it's my turn," he grinned at her over his shoulder.

Angrily, she fell to with a will, scrubbing his back until he flinched. "Easy, sweet," he said. "You will have the hide off me."

"It is no more than you deserve," she hissed, turning to swim away.

"We aren't finished, pet," he laughed, reaching out an arm to pull her back. "Your front needs attention."

"Let me go!" she spat. "If you don't, I'll scream."

"Scream away," he chuckled, holding her immobile with an arm about her waist. "No Turk would intervene between a man and his *guzdeh*. Do you know what that means, my sweet? Ibrahim tells me it is a maiden who has caught her master's eye, but hasn't yet been summoned to his bed. Don't squirm so. How can I bathe you if you won't hold still."

"Oh!" she stormed, then found herself going limp when he lathered the soap over his stomach and her breasts. He took particular pains with her breasts, cupping them and teasing the nipples with his thumbs until she sagged against him and unknowingly wiggled her bottom against his loins.

He gasped and released her. "Swim around until I've finished," he said, industriously lathering his chest. "I won't be long."

Natia luxuriated in the feel of the water on her bare skin and in a moment was happily splashing about in the pool. Suddenly a hand grabbed an ankle and pulled her under. When they broke the surface she was locked in his embrace, her breasts rousing his passions with their peaks teasing against his chest. His hands slid down to her bottom and he crushed her to him with her buttocks held in his hands. His lips left her mouth and went to the hollow at the base of her throat, causing her to tremble. "You would tempt a saint," he said, raising his head to stare down at her breasts only partially concealed by the water. "In fact, my love, I'm considering taking you on yonder bank."

"You wouldn't!" she gasped, striving to pull away from him. "I am not an animal, to be mounted in the grass!"

His eyes widened and he could not help but laugh. "Where did you learn such language?" he asked, still chuckling.

"My father bred horses," she replied, jerking free. "I've seen the way of a stallion with a mare. Thank you, no. It will be decently in a bed, or not at all."

"There are more places to make love than in a bed, my sweet. It will be my pleasure to show you."

"How can you have the affrontery to remark about my remark with a remark that is much worse than my remark!" she demanded.

A gleam came into his eyes and he heard himself say: "I did not intend that my remark should be worse than your remark when I remarked about your remark."

"Oh! You beast!" she breathed, thoroughly intending to storm away with her dignity still intact. Alas, the water. She could only flounder through it to the bank, his laughter trailing in her wake. Unaware she was treating him to an enticing view of her posterior, she scrambled ashore and looked about for a place to dress. Spying a large clump of fern, she scooped up her clothing and dashed behind it.

Grinning to himself, he swam to the bank and vaulted out. "Take your time, sweet," he drawled in the general direction of the fern, and calmly set about the task of toweling himself dry.

The sound of his voice caused her to peep through the foliage. Again she could not help but look; fascinated, she continued to stare while her body dried of its own accord. Later she wondered if he knew; he certainly took his time about it, she thought. But that was much later. For now, she gazed at the muscles rippling with each movement he made, her eyes coming at last to rest on his manhood. Only when he was fully clothed did she think to dress herself.

CHAPTER SIX

As Ibrahim had predicted, Devon and Natia were made welcome by the tribesmen. Following a conference at which everyone seemed to join in, two riders set off at a gallop in search of the *Seahawk* with a message for Riafat and Marston to remain aboard. Those left behind stuffed themselves with roast meat and stretched out under the shade of palm trees to rest from the scorching heat of the midday sun. Devon spread his burnous upon the ground for Natia and lay down beside her. Within moments they were fast asleep.

It seemed they had scarcely closed their eyes when Ibrahim shook them awake. "I will leave you now," he said. "My people will take you to my uncle. Do not be surprised to find you are traveling east. You will circle around Damascus before turning south. I doubt the Janissaries would accost you even if they stumbled upon you, but it is foolish to tempt fate."

"Why wouldn't they?" Devon asked, helping Natia to her feet.

"The tribe of my uncle numbers some two hundred twenty-five thousand souls spread over some thirty-six thousand square miles. For the most part we are left in peace, unmolested by other tribes and treated with grudging respect by emissaries of the Sultan. Everyone knows the magnificent Arabian horses we breed are prized in Constantinople. Even the Janissaries keep their distance."

"God grant that they do!" Devon replied from the bottom of his heart.

Ibrahim's eyes twinkled. "If Allah wills it, my lord," he said.

A tribesman came forward leading a mare by her bridle. "You must ride double, Master," he said, grinning. "We breeders of horses for our Sheik have no spare among us. I have placed a cushion for your lady so she may ride behind you."

Devon threw back his head and laughed. "When you know my lady better, you will know to place her cushion before me," he told the surprised tribesman. "What is your name?"

"It is Ali, Master."

"Well, Ali, I am not your master. Call me Devon. It is my name. I have been meaning to ask someone how it is all of you speak English.

"The grandfather of our mighty Sheik studied in your England when he was young. Since then, all boy children of our tribe must speak the language by the time they reach puberty."

"What of the girl children?" Devon asked, cutting his eyes to Natia.

Ali shrugged. "They need only know how to please a man."

Natia held her tongue and refused to meet Devon's eyes as he swung aboard the mare and reached down a hand. Settling herself before him, she attempted to ignore the provocative remarks issuing from his mouth. She kept her face straight ahead, pretending to hear not one word.

The tribesman who appeared to be in charge raised an arm, and the entire group sent their horses plunging forward. Natia fully expected they would slow the pace, but it soon became apparent they were accustomed to riding at full gallop. It was only after several miles were covered that she realized both horse and man preferred it that way.

They had early formed a double column, with the leader out in front and Devon and Natia bringing up the rear. The reins were in his right hand and his left arm encircled her waist. "Lean against me, sweetheart," his voice murmured in her ear. "Unless I'm much mistaken, they will keep this up all afternoon."

Natia realized her body was tense without her being aware of it. She forced herself to relax and settled back against his chest. It wasn't to be expected that he could remain aloof to the soft curves so close to his hand. Nor could he. The hand slipped inside her burnous and boldly cupped a breast. When she made no protest, he grinned and left it there.

They slept that night out under the stars, each rolled up in his burnous. It had been a long and tiring day; Natia somehow found the strength to eat the cold meat Devon pressed into her hand, and then was ready to lie down. Warned by Ali that the desert can become cold at night, he spread her burnous on top of his, lay down beside her, and wrapped the covering around them.

By early afternoon of the following day they had circled around the city of Damascus and were heading south. The horses never seemed to tire; once they settled into the rhythm of a gallop, they went on and on, fairly eating up the miles. Natia no longer rode astride. When she sat down during the noonday pause, Devon had seen her wince. Knowing her bottom was sore, he now held her across his lap with her face cradled in his throat.

Just upon dusk they reached their destination. At least two hundred tents were pitched around a huge oasis, the largest one off to one side a short distance from the others. The tribesmen wound their way through the camp and drew to a halt before the tent of the Sheik. He was certainly alerted to their coming. It seemed that half of the adults, and all of the children, had followed the procession, drawn by the presence of Natia and Devon. The babble became deafening, but died away immediately their leader stepped through the open flap of his tent and held up a hand for silence.

"I, Sheik Abdullah den Kallaj, am honored to welcome Lord and Lady Devon to my camp," he bowed, salaaming. "Be pleased to step inside."

His was a commanding presence, tall and lean and dark, with only a touch of gray at his temples and powdering his pointed beard. Devon had no trouble at all in understanding the awe with which his people regarded him.

The tent was spacious, its interior divided into several rooms by woven hangings which served as walls. Low, comfortable divans stood about the reception room, interspersed with tables of beaten brass; the floor was covered with luxuriant Persian rugs.

The Sheik clapped his hands and a procession of servants entered bearing trays of sweet cakes, cool drinks, and cups of a strong, black brew. Natia had tasted Turkish coffee and thought it bitter, so she accepted a cup of fruit juice and sat down upon a divan. Devon opted for the coffee and sat down beside her.

"Ibrahim sent word of your coming," the Sheik said. "The Sultan may wield great power in his part of the world but here he is of less importance than a single grain of sand. This is the time of year when our people move southward for better grazing for the horses. You are welcome to remain with us until we reach the Barada. Ibrahim's courier informed us your yacht is waiting there."

"Your generosity is appreciated and most welcome,

Highness," Devon replied. "We would not get far on our own, I'm sure."

"You would perhaps wish word sent to your ship? It cannot be safe to drop anchor in the river each and every night. A camp as large as ours moves slowly, my lord. Thirty moons will pass before you have need of her."

"Again, Your Highness, I can only thank you."

"It will be done. You have little to thank me for, my lord. Riafat's father was our younger brother. Vengeance can taste sweet on the tongue. You are tired; I will not detain you," he added, rising. "A tent has been prepared for you. I trust it will suit your needs."

Devon and Natia uttered the appropriate words and followed a servant to a tent pitched a short distance away. It was as luxuriously appointed as the Sheik's, though of a smaller size. Natia gazed about in delight. The Persian rugs beneath their feet echoed the colors of silk and velvet cushions scattered about the room, a low table of wood inlaid with ivory stood before the divan, and shining brass lamps hung suspended on metal chains encased in velvet.

A serving girl came forward to relieve Natia of her burnous, and indicated she was to sit on the floor. She did so, knowing full well the harem costume revealed a good deal more of her body than it concealed, then regretted her compliance when Devon was seated on the divan. A second serving girl placed a bowl of water on the floor and dropped to her knees before him. First she wiped his hands with a damp cloth and dried them with a square of linen. Next she removed his soft leather shoes and cleansed his feet in the same way. Natia unaccountably became very interested in smoothing the thin gauze that covered her knees, determined not to look at him. The next moments were to sorely try her patience.

Dinner was brought to Devon by women who knelt

at his feet, each with a bowl in her hands. One proffered lamb kebobs arranged on a silver platter, the other held forward a spicy pilaf for him to scoop up in his fingers. His hands were washed again when he had eaten, he was handed a cup of coffee, and the servants withdrew, leaving the remains of the meal for Natia.

Silence reigned supreme. For two full minutes neither of them moved or spoke. Then Devon threw back his head and laughed, the room ringing with his chuckles. "Let that be a lesson to you," he said when he was able.

Natia rose in one graceful movement. "I am aware you find it funny," she said levelly, "but if you think that I will feed you, think again, sir!"

"Come here," he invited, his eyes still brimful with amusement.

"So!" she shot back. "My lord and master speaks!"

"Sit down, sweet," he grinned, reaching for her hand. "The food is delicious."

She thrust out her lower lip. "I'm not hungry," she said.

"Yes, you are," he contradicted, scooping up pilaf in his fingers. "Open your mouth."

"Are you pretending?" she asked, eyeing him doubtfully.

A devilish glint came into his eyes. "A slave serves his mistress," he said. "Open up."

The humor of it struck her. "You haven't washed my feet," she said with a perfectly straight face.

He was not to be bested. "Eat your dinner like a good girl, and I will wash more than your feet before I tuck you in yonder bed."

Natia looked around in surprise. In another room, and barely visible behind hangings of thinnest gauze, a sleeping couch stood against a wall, illuminated by soft candlelight. She blushed.

"The sooner you eat, the sooner you sleep," he remarked.

Natia decided she was being childish and accepted the food from his fingers. She insisted she feed herself, but he wouldn't hear of it, so she collapsed in giggles and let him poke the morsels into her mouth. "I will grow fat and lazy," she remarked when she could eat no more.

He looked up from dipping his fingers into the basin of water. "You need exercise," he grinned, drying his hands on the square of linen.

"Yes, my lord," she twinkled demurely, and dropped her eyes.

He leaned back and took her in his arms, holding her carefully. "When you look at me like that, my love, I am sore pressed," he murmured against her hair. The scent of her, the softness of her body, sent a surge of desire stabbing through him. Then she turned her face up to his and their lips met. He meant it to be a brief expression of affection, but her arms crept around his neck and the kiss lengthened.

"Natia, darling Natia," he groaned. "You are so beautiful, so incredibly beautiful. You drive me to the edge of madness."

"Don't stop," she breathed against his lips. "Please don't stop. Kiss me again."

"Do you realize what will happen if I do?" he said, staring into her eyes. "I promised it would be on the yacht. If I kiss you again—"

"Who cares for promises," she murmured, pressing against him. "It is lovely here. Kiss me."

His mouth clamped on hers, his lips bruising hers as he kissed her deeply, hungrily, the restraint he had clamped over himself for days falling away. Natia trembled with the violence of his passion and gave herself over to the sensations he was rousing in her, scarcely aware of the half-intelligible words of love he whispered in her ear. "Natia, Natia, I have wanted you so," he murmured, pressing burning kisses on her mouth and throat, the warmth of her response fanning the flame within him until, with a groan, he lifted her in his arms and carried her to the bed waiting in the candlelight.

He lay her down against the pillows and bent over her, his fingers trailing over her face and throat to the clasp holding the two halves of her jacket together. She flushed slightly when he removed it and blushed rosily when he untied the sash at her waist and pulled the harem trousers down over her hips and from her feet.

His breath catching in his throat, he rose to strip away his clothing, his eyes sweeping over her body, caressing the soft curves. Natia smiled softly and held out her arms and drew him down to her. Reaching up, he loosened her hair and spread it over her shoulders, stroking the silken strands. "My darling, my Natia, my precious Natia," he murmured, pressing his lips to the pulse throbbing in her throat. "I adore you, I want you, but I'm afraid of frightening you."

Her fingers wound through his hair, and she cradled his head against her breasts. "You could never frighten me," she whispered. "I want you to love me—any way you—wish."

She heard the quick intake of his breath, and then he was above her, pressing her down into the pillows. He gazed at her a moment, his eyes gone dark with passion, before his lips swooped on hers. He was slow and careful, his voice soothing in her ears, his hands gentle on her body, until, when at last she became one with him, pleasure mingled with the pain and only joy remained.

The candle flame sputtered in its pool of wax and flickered out, leaving the pair entwined within the bed in darkness. Natia lay asleep in Devon's arms, her head resting on his shoulder and a dreamy half-smile curving her lips. He held her tenderly, pro-

tectively, as he had never before held any woman.
How often he had pictured her as she was now, her
skin moist and slightly flushed in the aftermath of
his lovemaking. Suddenly he hungered for her kisses,
ached to lose himself within her warmth.

Gently removing his arms, he eased himself from
the bed and rose to kindle the flame of a candle. She
lay on her back, her lashes a sooty fringe against her
cheeks, her hair a rioting of golden curls against the
pillows. His breath catching in his throat, his eyes ran
over her naked body, feasted on pink-tipped breasts
and silken thighs. Unable to contain himself longer,
he sat down upon the bed, his hands sweeping over
her in one long caress. "Natia!" his breath whispered
in her ear. "Wake up, my darling."

Her eyes flew open and she stared at him, momentarily dazed. "Oh!" she said foolishly. "Are you
awake?"

"My love, my heart, how can I sleep?" he groaned,
crushing her in his arms. "I want you—now. I don't
think I can bear to wait. Do you—"

"Need you ask?" she murmured softly, slipping her
arms about his neck and pressing her breasts against
his chest.

He trembled above her, kissing her and murmuring
soft words of love until, his manhood deep within her,
she cried out to him in her need and rose to meet his
thrusts. His eyes widened at her response, and he
gloried in his triumph as she gave herself wholly to
him, her passion flaming to meet his until their souls
touched and they found the ultimate joy together.
Wordlessly he collapsed in her embrace, the tears
stinging his eyelids in the splendor of it.

CHAPTER SEVEN

To one unaccustomed to the sounds of an awakening Bedouin camp, the chatter of women's voices as they set about the task of cooking the morning meal over charcoal braziers and the laughter of children tumbling about their feet in play proved irresistible. Smiling, Natia raised her head and gazed at Devon sleeping peacefully by her side. In repose he appeared vulnerable, more a boy than the man of strength and courage she knew him to be. With his eyes closed, she was able to leisurely study his features unhampered by his penetrating gaze. Her eyes moved from the arch of his eyebrows to the thick fringe of lashes against his cheeks, and down the proud nose to the generous mouth sweetly curving over even white teeth. How handsome he is, she thought, her gaze roaming from his tanned face to his raven hair, her fingers itching to bury themselves in the curling locks.

"Why aren't you sleeping," his voice spoke, causing her to give a little jump. "Could the absence of my kisses be keeping you awake?"

Startled brown eyes met amused blue ones. "If you prefer me asleep, then by all means, kiss me," she returned pertly. "Do you mean to kiss me?"

"Don't quibble," he grinned, pulling her forward to lie across his chest.

"If you don't care to kiss me, I won't press you," she assured him, tracing a finger over his lips. "Nothing is more disagreeable than being urged to do something one doesn't care to do. You needn't explain that to me. Are you going to kiss me?"

Chuckling, he rolled over with her and sought the hollow at the base of her throat with his lips. "Beware, my sweet. You're too damned beautiful," he murmured, enjoying the feel of her bare flesh against his skin. "Unless you want me to commit mayhem upon this luscious body of yours, you will reform your ways."

"For all I know, it could be a lovely way to start the day," she replied, laughing gaily.

His lips were very close to hers. "I love you, Natia," he said, his eyes suddenly serious. "I mean to spend the rest of my life proving it to you."

"Colin!" she gasped, shocked. "Even Nurse would never talk like that! Proving it to me, indeed! As if you haven't risked your life—Oh, my God! Nurse!"

"She is safe, and waiting for us on the *Seahawk*. Don't cry, dearest. You will ruin your pretty eyes."

"I feel so guilty," she gulped, stricken. "Colin, I had forgotten all about her!"

"You have had almost more on your mind than it could bear. Do not imagine that you are heartless, Natia. Anyone would suppose you have been having a gay time of it."

"The truth of it is, I have," she admitted, adding quickly: "Except for the one episode, of course. However did you manage to rescue Nurse?"

"It was simple, really. Riafat merely bought her at public auction."

Her laughter bubbled over. "I'm strongly of the opinion he will live to regret it," she gurgled. "I promise you Nurse will have her bristles up."

"On the contrary," he protested, his lip quivering. "She displayed a commendable degree of appreciation. As for you, fair torment—"

She cocked her head. "Well?" she prompted.

"Surely you aren't intending to lay claim to a sensibility equaling Nurse's?" he grinned, and nuzzled at her throat.

"That is exactly what I do intend. No, you needn't show your teeth. Whatever have I done to deserve a scold?"

"What haven't you done?" he murmured, distributing little nibbling kisses across her cheek. "You bared your breasts before me and flaunted your round bottom before my eyes until I thought I would die of it. God! What didn't you do?"

Natia opened her mouth to reply, then closed it again upon hearing a murmur of voices entering the tent. "Damnation!" Devon swore softly under his breath. Rising, he pulled on his breeches. "I will find you something decent to wear," he said, parting the curtains to go into the other room.

Natia pulled the sheet to her chin. Since Ibrahim had told them women of the tribe were unschooled in languages, she knew he would seek the tent of the Sheik. Hoping he would find something other than the shapeless garments she had seen around the camp, she rolled over and closed her eyes. She would never have imagined it possible that she could find herself miles from civilization with nothing to wear. Idly wondering if some pirate's wench now strolled about in her own lost finery, she drifted into sleep.

A hand on her shoulder awakened her, and she looked up to see a Bedouin woman standing by the bed. She held out a European-style gown and made a gesture for Natia to put it on. It soon become apparent her knowledge of Western dress was almost nonexistent. Try as she would, Natia could not make the woman understand the need for undergarments.

Sighing, she gave it up and slipped the gown on over her head. It was not in the latest mode, having very full skirts, but at least the bodice fastened down the front. Natia managed the buttons without assistance and went into the other room. Fresh baked bread, fruit, and a pitcher of goat's milk were brought to her, but she was not surprised when no one came forward to serve her. She especially enjoyed the crusty bread, but found she could not drink the milk. Finished, she rose and crossed to the flap of the tent.

A tinker's cart standing a short distance away was surrounded by a group of chattering women haggling over the worth of a needle and the price of a spool of thread. Natia caught sight of Devon standing head and shoulders above them all and joined him in time to add a mirror of polished steel and a ball of scented soap to his purchases. Delighted to possess a comb and brush, and even a tiny vial of perfume, she hurried back to the tent. She had some difficulty in making the servant understand her wants, but finally a basin of water and a cloth were brought to her, and she enjoyed the luxury of washing with the scented soap. Next she hung the mirror from a peg protruding from a tent pole and did up her hair. Satisfied with her improved appearance, she touched her throat with a drop of the perfume, carefully arranged the comb and brush upon a chest, and went into the other room to join Devon.

"Um," he breathed, pulling her into his arms. "You smell nice."

"I did the best I could, but I would feel much more civilized if I had some underclothing."

He stared down at her, amused. "Are you saying the women brought you nothing to wear under your gown?" he grinned.

"I couldn't seem to make them understand. Perhaps you could speak to the Sheik?"

"And spoil my fun? Certainly not!" He added, chuckling; "Perhaps it may come in handy."

"And again, perhaps it won't!" she shot back.

"We will go into that later," he said, releasing her to pick up a burnous. "The Sheik has offered to show me his horses."

"May I go with you?"

"If it were up to me, you could. As it is, I shouldn't advise we introduce Christian innovations into the camp. I know that look," he added, alarmed. "Whatever you are thinking, I trust you won't act upon it."

She showed him a face of sweet innocence. "I am not a Bedouin woman," she said.

"If that was meant to pacify me, it doesn't. What mischief are you planning?"

"That," she said sweetly, "need not concern you."

"The devil!" he exclaimed, frowning. "Out with it, my girl, before I shake you."

"Women need to be treated with kindness, Colin. They—well, never mind. I doubt I could explain it to you."

"Natia, I don't know whether dinner last evening put some idea into your head, or whether it is a notion you have hatched for my benefit, but you will listen to me. Meddling in the customs of these people could lead you into danger. You could receive a severe beating; you might even have salt rubbed into the wounds. Only recall what you have already endured, if you think I am exaggerating."

"Well, I must say that takes a load off my mind," she gurgled, her laughter bubbling over. "I was afraid, seeing you with a burnous over your arm, that you were going native."

"It would serve you right if I did," he said, his stern expression giving way to a smile. "And that brings me to the reason for the burnous. The Sheik requests we wear one every time we leave our tent. Allah wills it. And it will help disguise you."

"Are you hoaxing me?"

"I am not. While the foot of the camel tramples the righteous, evil rides on the wings of birds to the dove-cote of the wicked."

"Colin!"

"I don't wonder you are astounded; I was myself, until I thought about it. The desert only seems vast and empty, my dear; never ride out unaccompanied."

"No, I see it wouldn't be a wise thing to do. What, pray, am I expected to ride?"

"Did I neglect to tell you?" he asked teasingly. "It must have slipped my mind. The Sheik has promised to put two horses at our disposal."

"His finest, I trust?"

There was undisguised provocation in her voice, but the only response it drew from him was a chuckle as he blew her a kiss and vanished through the flap of the tent.

With nothing to occupy her time, Natia wandered about the room, touching a bowl intricately enameled in blue and white, and lightly running her fingers over a chair. Finally she went into the other room and lay down upon the couch. She could not remember when she had felt so alone, nor had she realized how much she had come to rely on Devon. How could she not have known that a languid, faintly mocking exquisite in laced and scented coats could own a courage beyond that of ordinary men, and a will of steel to back it up. She had heard the respect in the Sheik's voice when he spoke to Devon, but in her ignorance she was only now coming to appreciate the risks he had taken in rescuing her from her own folly. He must love me very much, she mused, and drifted into sleep on the thought.

Sometime later his voice calling to her as he strode into the tent awakened her. Before she could scarcely more than blink, he had bundled her into a burnous and led her outside. "Oh!" she breathed, gazing at the most magnificent coal-black mare she had ever seen.

"The Sheik tells me she is descended from a strain that goes back to the days of Sulieman. Do you think you can manage her?"

"I'm sure I can," she replied, placing her foot in his locked hands to mount herself. "She is gentle. I can see it in her eyes," she called over her shoulder as the mare bounded forward at her touch and broke into a gallop.

Surprised cries rose in her wake. She heard thudding hooves coming up fast behind her, and a moment later Devon was beside her, trailed by an escort of grinning tribesmen. "What the hell do you think you're doing?" he demanded, fear making his voice raw.

She cut her eyes to him and said, "My father bred horses with mettle, Colin. I will inform you that he withheld comment on the way I rode."

"I am not your father," he shot back, lips grim.

"Fortunately," she teased, and gave her entrancing gurgle of laughter.

Eyeing her profile, he said, somewhat inadequately, "Don't think you will succeed in fobbing me off, for you won't." When she did not reply, he gave it up.

They galloped on for some time before Devon, acting on a nod from Ali, reached out a hand for the mare's bridle and turned them in the direction of a patch of green some distance off to the left. It was small for an oasis, consisting of a few palm trees clustered about a well; but the shade was welcome, and the water cool. Sentries were posted, the horses tethered, and everyone lay down to rest. Suddenly the sentries were among them, speaking in urgent whispers and pointing to a cloud of dust approaching from the east. In a very few minutes the horses had been led away behind a large dune where they would be out of hearing as well as sight, and the entire party lay stretched out on the sand hidden behind another dune, their guns ready in their hands.

Natia had never been so terrified. The tension was intolerable, and the tribesmen were holding their breaths lest some slight sound betray their presence. No one had explained it to her, but she knew the riders must be a murderous band of cutthroats for the Sheik's men to react as they had. Every sound the marauders made was clearly audible. She heard them ride in and could follow their movements from the moment they drew water from the well until they lay down to rest. They laughed and joked among themselves, but their voices sounded coarse and cruel and sent a shiver down her spine. Time dragged by and still they waited, seared by a broiling sun and almost afraid to breathe. Natia's gaze locked with Devon's; his lips formed a silent kiss, and she summoned up a smile. Suddenly the tribesmen seemed to tense; sounds of horses' hooves moving through the trees came clearly to their ears. A blood-curdling shout rent the air, and within minutes the brigands had galloped out of sight in the direction from whence they came.

"Allah be praised, her ladyship is safe," Ali murmured, getting to his feet.

"Who were they?" Devon asked, reaching down a hand to Natia.

"The offal from many tribes, my lord. Their own people cast them out, so they band together and prey on the unwary. They are much feared, but one day Allah will drive them from our lands."

"I sincerely hope so," Natia said. "I was never so frightened."

"They must be always on the move, my lady. We will see no more of them. Even so, it is better we return to camp."

That evening, much to Natia's surprise, they both received an invitation to dine with the Sheik. He received them seated on a chair that looked very much like the thrones which she had read about in her history books. As wide as a sofa, it had four short posts much like a bed and was encrusted with mother-of-pearl. A chair with its seat fairly high off the floor had been placed on the Sheik's right, while the seat of the chair on his left was much closer to the floor. Natia was not at all surprised to find herself conducted to the latter.

The Sheik clapped his hands and the curtains at the side of the room parted to admit a dwarf who approached his master on his knees. He was followed immediately by a procession of servants bearing food on trays. One by one they paused for the dwarf to taste each dish for poison before presenting it to the men, a procedure that was purely ritual and reserved for state occasions. Natia sat quietly and waited, her face expressionless, while the Sheik and Devon ate before the servants offered the trays to her. She debated the folly of refusing for a moment, and then, knowing she would only go to bed hungry, ate sparingly from a number of them.

The meal concluded, a slave appeared at her elbow to usher her from the tent. Natia didn't trust herself to speak. She sketched her host a shallow curtsy—an insult in itself and one which went completely over his head, much to Devon's relief—and went from the room with her head held high. The sight of musicians hidden behind a screen, and scantily clad dancing girls awaiting the summons to entertain, did nothing to cool her temper. Pausing before her own tent, she stood gazing at the stars to calm herself before going inside to bed.

The moon had set when Devon entered and stood gazing down at her. She lay on her side curled up into a ball, with her hands tucked under her chin. Desire for her rose up in him, but the hour was late and he hadn't the heart to awaken her. Stripping off his clothing, he could only marvel at himself. Never before had he turned away from the passion bedeviling him out of consideration for any woman. Clearly he was bewitched.

"So!" her voice spoke, startling him. "My lord and master deigns to join me!"

Devon sat down upon the bed, chuckling. "Did you think I wouldn't, foolish girl?" he murmured, reaching for her.

"Don't touch me!" she cried, her brown eyes ablaze with sudden anger. "You smell of—of a harem!"

He stared at her in amazement, surprised at the outburst. "I smell of incense, sweetheart, and devilish unpleasant it was, believe me."

"Hah!" she snorted. "I saw the dancing girls. Next you will say you didn't look!"

"Of course I looked. How could I help it? They were right before my eyes."

Natia considered this. "Were they—shapely?" she asked, her eyes brimming with mischief as suddenly as they had become irate.

"There was a time when I would have thought so," he said obligingly, gathering her into his arms. Unable to wait longer, he pulled her into position beneath him and fastened his lips on hers.

CHAPTER EIGHT

In the weeks ahead they came to understand the Bedouin tribesmen as few outsiders might. Natia quickly saw that the women, far from being subservient, actually ruled their husbands with a firm if subtle hand. The men, secretly fearing rejection by their wives, cultivated an outward appearance of fierce superiority which bolstered their ego before their fellows, but which they shed like a second skin upon entering their tents at night. The children enjoyed the best of both worlds, being loved and cosseted by one and all. More than once Natia saw a child caught up and comforted for some minor hurt by whoever happened to be handy at the moment.

As time passed Natia and Devon came to know one another as few of their own world might. Thrown much in each other's company by circumstances, they talked of many things together until each knew the other's mind as well as he knew his own. Friends as well as lovers, they moved through companionship-filled days in anticipation of passion-filled nights when their lovemaking left them breathless and close as few couples of any age are privileged to be. Natia satisfied Devon's every desire, and she was content to bask in his love, each of them without thought of having their idyll end.

One morning, after they had been with the Bedouins a month, a tribesman rode into the camp at breakneck speed, flung himself from his lathered horse, and ran to the tent of the Sheik. Within minutes Devon received a summons, and Natia, agog with curiosity, sat down to wait. Time seemed to her to drag, though actually less than five minutes elapsed before he returned. She had risen to her feet when he walked in, and her eyes were on his questioningly as he strode across to her. "Put this on," he instructed, stripping off his shirt.

"What on earth!" she exclaimed, eyeing the shapeless blue garment he'd thrust into her hand.

"The soldiers are less than an hour away," he replied, peeling off his trousers. "The tinker saw us here and reported it."

"How can you possibly know that?"

"He is with them. The sentry saw him. For God's sake, Natia, don't argue."

"I still don't see—"

"The wife of one of the tribesmen is a blonde from Germany. She will play your role. The Sheik is scouring the camp at this moment for someone who can pass for me. Count your blessings, sweet. The scene the soldiers will be called upon to witness will be amorous in the extreme."

"Colin!" she gasped, shocked. "You can't mean—"

He was on her in two strides. Before she could protest, he pulled her gown from her body and over her head. "Later," he murmured, and turned away to dress himself in the manner of the tribesmen. No sooner was he clothed than servants entered with the blonde from Germany and a man whose height approximated Devon's. Natia was dressed, her eyes painted with kohl, her hair and features hidden beneath smothering veils with only her eyes showing.

She was led forth to squat in the shade with the elderly women of the tribe, a shapeless lump indistinguishable from other shapeless lumps. Peeping from under her lashes, she saw Devon lose himself among the tribesmen grooming horses some distance away.

The soldiers were first seen on the horizon as a cloud of dust, and then as a double row of horsemen trailed some distance behind by the tinker in his cart. To the untrained eye, the camp seemed much as always, but the skilled observer would have known that every eye was on the approaching riders. As was usual the children, who knew nothing of the plot, ran out to greet them and trailed along beside them to the tent of their leader. The tinker climbed down from his cart and swaggered forward just as the Sheik bowed a greeting to the Captain. "Welcome to our humble camp," he said, salaaming. "Be pleased to step inside. A refreshing drink goes well on such a day as this."

The Captain swung down from his horse and gave the order for his men to dismount. "You have a white-skinned houri hidden here," he said without preamble. "Produce her!"

The Sheik looked aggrieved. "You insult the tent of my ancestors!" he said. "I have no need to hide my women!"

"Not your woman, fool! The Sultan's!"

The Sheik bowed. "Perhaps Allah will see fit to untie your tongue," he remarked blandly.

"You!" the Captain growled, motioning the tinker forward. "This man reports she bought trinkets from his cart, as did the foreign devil by her side."

" 'Tis true, may Allah smite me dead," the tinker grinned, displaying rotting teeth. "A mirror of steel took her fancy, along with a comb for her golden hair."

A slight smile curved the Sheik's lips. "Allah in his wisdom has seen fit to unravel the many strands of yarn. You no doubt refer to my kinsman Mustaffi, and his newest goddess of delight. You will find them in yonder tent, though it would be cruel to interrupt his pleasure."

The Captain motioned for his men to take up position on either side of the flap in question and strode into the tent with the Sheik close upon his heels. The outer room was deserted, but clothing strewn across the floor led to draperies beyond which groans and gasps were clearly audible. The Captain kicked a garment from his path and jerked aside the curtains.

Long tapering legs encircled the waist of the man plunging into the soft white body pinned beneath him. Blond hair tossed upon the pillows as the woman's lithe body arched to meet him, moving rhythmically with his thrusts.

"Up!" the Captain growled, striking the man's bare backside with his palm.

The man turned his head as if startled, then scrambled to his feet, attempting to hide his swollen manhood with his hands. "By the beard of the Prophet, the Sultan grows careless of his subjects," he complained with a fine show of temper. "Has a free man no privacy?"

The Captain ignored him, his eyes running over the woman's body and coming to rest upon her face. "Bah!" he spat, disgusted. "This was no virgin of tender years! She is thirty if she's a day!"

"Did I not tell you?" the Sheik said. "Come, let us go, if you are satisfied. We keep Mustaffi from his labors."

Outside, the tinker waited impatiently for the reward he felt sure was within his grasp. He knew just how he would spend the money. A man needed a woman to cook his food and warm his bed. That one might also launder his clothing never occurred to him. Traveling around as he did, he seldom both-

ered to wash—the reason, no doubt, that he possessed
a woman only rarely.

Confident in his ignorance, he proudly approached
the Captain, who now stood a respectful step behind
the Sheik. "Is it not true you owe this worthless subject
of the Sultan a great debt?" he said, prostrating himself at the officer's feet.

"Silence, you offspring of the jackal!" the Captain
roared. "You have insulted our Great Sultan with
your greed and wasted my time with your lies. I
shall not kill you, though you will plead for death
before I'm through."

The tinker blanched deathly white as the Captain
spoke, and desperately searched his mind for the cause.
"The *gedikli*, Master?" he quavered, terrified.

"Fool! Spawn of darkness! Did you think to foist an
aging harlot on His Supreme Highness? Seize him!"

For a moment the camp seemed to hold its collec-
tive breath, then released it on a sigh as the Captain's
second-in-command laid hold of the tinker and dragged
him screaming from the scene. The Captain then
bowed to the Sheik, rapped out an order to his men,
and swung aboard his horse. Natia, surreptitious witness to the drama, went weak with relief, the tears
starting from her eyes. The old woman squatting beside her touched her arm in warning and she obediently bent her head, screening her face from view.

The tribesmen waited until the soldiers were clear
of the camp before riding in pursuit. Natia, now free
to watch, wondered at their intent as they swept past
the troop and galloped on until they were some distance ahead. Then to her utter astonishment they
wheeled their horses as one man and galloped back
toward the soldiers at top speed. They held their
bridles in their teeth, freeing their hands to brandish
long, curved swords, and to fire their pistols into the
air. Natia thought they must surely fall and be tram-

pled when they threw themselves under the bellies of their horses, but they swung back into their saddles, the most blood-curdling war cries issuing from their throats. Just when she feared they must crash into the soldiers, they pulled their mounts back on their haunches and formed a single line strung out before the Sultan's men. It was a brilliant display of horsemanship, but the Captain was in no mood to appreciate it. Obliged to alter his course to detour his troop around the grinning tribesmen, the set of his lips augured ill for the hapless tinker tied to the end of a rope and stumbling along on swollen feet.

Finally the last soldier vanished from view over the horizon, the dust settled, and Devon was at her side. Helping her to her feet, he said, "It will be politic on our part to return to our tent. These people can't take much joy from the sight of us."

"Why?" she asked, hurrying to keep pace with him.

"Muslim views on adultery are at least as strict as our own," he replied, fitting his stride to her shorter step. "A man may honor a guest by lending him the services of a concubine, but a wife must remain faithful to her husband."

"Oh!" she said, digesting this. "Well, it isn't so very different with us, is it?"

Devon held back the flap for her to enter the tent and did not reply. She crossed the room to remove her veil, observing as she did so her gown laid out neatly over a chair. The unknown blonde, then, had not worn it. "I'm surprised she didn't," she remarked, turning to face him.

Devon looked startled. "I am not usually dull-witted, but—I don't take your meaning."

"My gown. She didn't wear it."

He looked amused. "Yes, I see she didn't."

"It is rather difficult to explain, Colin, but I wouldn't have wanted a concubine wearing it. I expect you will be horribly shocked, but I wouldn't have minded if it were a wife."

"That is perfectly understandable," he remarked, lips twitching.

"I'm sorry to have to say it, but I would feel the same if it were your mistress. I certainly wouldn't lend her my clothing."

"No," he said with perfect gravity. "I expect you wouldn't."

"Some men," she continued, "expect a wife to turn her head while he—"

"Cavorts far from the nest? May I know whether I am being cast in this disagreeable light?"

"Oh, no!" she said earnestly. "It is just that we were speaking of the Muslims, and I think women are treated in much the same way at home. Don't you?"

"I really hadn't thought about it."

"Women only want to be treated as equals."

"I'm sure they do."

"We really have very good minds, you know. Most men resent the fact that we are capable of looking after ourselves."

"Most men, my dear, are well aware they dance to their lady's tune. How did we get off on this subject?"

"Well, you did say the men here loan their concubines to friends, and I only thought the men at home pass their mistresses back and forth in much the same way."

"I wouldn't phrase it quite like that, but perhaps you are right. I still don't see what this has to do with you."

"I'm trying to explain it to you," she said, wrinkling her brow. "You see, when a woman hasn't a husband to take care of her, she must fend for herself. The trouble is, men won't hire her because they think she hasn't a brain. There is nothing left for her to do but become some man's mistress."

"To them, a life of ease is infinitely preferable to a life of toil, my dear."

"As to that, I couldn't say. I haven't talked to one." Seeing the expression on his face, she added hastily: "Not that I intend to."

"You comfort me," he said.

She drew closer. "I have decided there is something we must do," she began in pleading accents. "We must start a school for impoverished young females."

"Good God!" he said blankly.

She took a deep breath and continued: "I am sure they could be taught to work in an office. Women often write with a pretty hand, and anyone can learn to enter numbers on a page. But you know all about that, I'm sure."

At that a laugh escaped him. "Surely you don't envision me in the role of headmaster," he said.

"I only meant you have a secretary, silly."

"And where do you plan to locate this school of yours?"

"In London, I think. Do you own a property there?"

"I own several properties there, my dear."

"Good! It is settled, then. Just think, Colin. If we had never spent so much time with these people, I might never have thought of it."

He reached out his hand, and when she put hers into it, he said, "I will agree on one condition, Natia. You are not to neglect me."

Her eyes began to dance. "I don't plan to, sir, but I will make you no promises."

"Shall we seal our bargain with a kiss?" he returned, a glint in his eye.

This suggestion so met with her approval that she flung her arms around his neck and rubbed teasingly against him. His arms tightened around her, and he was kissing her as if he never meant to stop. Ali, coming quietly into the room, gaped in astonishment, then backed from the tent before his presence could be suspected. Grinning, he cleared his throat several times before going back into the room. Devon was now standing facing the entrance, but Natia had snatched her gown from the chair and whisked herself behind the curtains.

"I bring welcome news, my lord," Ali said, salaaming. "We travel south with the dawn."

"With the dawn!" Devon ejaculated, stunned. "Are you saying a camp the size of this one can pack so quickly?"

"When the time comes for the tribe to move, my lord, we must act swiftly. The reason can be the water, or locusts, or even boredom."

"What is it this time?"

"Our scouts report the raiders at the well have remained in the vicinity. They creep in under cover of darkness to rob and plunder; we have lost horses to them before. And now, it is time I go. You have no need to strike your tent, my lord. Someone will do it for you."

Natia and Devon were up and dressed the following morning by the time most of the tribesmen stumbled from their tents and set about the business of breaking camp. Each had his job to do and accomplished it with a minimum of fuss. The tents and rugs were lashed to the humps of camels, while smaller objects were loaded on the backs of pack-horses. The children and elderly members of the tribe found a seat on top of the bundles, but the younger men and women rode the magnificent Arabians. The caravan set off under a clear blue sky and a blazing sun. Natia and Devon rode at the head of the column beside the Sheik and the more important elders of the tribe. Next came the horses, and behind them the camels and pack-horses. Last in line, and several miles to the rear, shepherds herded the flocks of sheep and goats.

The day was growing warm and Natia, swathed in the enveloping burnous, began to long for the cooler fields of Devon Hall.

They stopped at noon to eat and rest. Natia had anticipated an oasis, but none appeared on the horizon. They simply paused where they were, canopies were set up to shelter the tribe from the sun, and everyone lay down in the shade. Two hours later the canopies were dismantled, everyone mounted, and they moved on. In late afternoon they stopped again, and an encampment of sorts was set up. The Sheik's tent was pitched, as was Natia and Devon's, but everyone else preferred sleeping in the open to the effort involved in raising theirs. They were invited to dine with the Sheik again; Natia was treated as an equal, the result, Devon informed her later in the privacy of their bed, of the Sheik's appreciation of her equestrian skills. The Sheik might now accord her the status of a man, but he labored under no such notion, he told her between kisses, and proceeded to prove his point. Most satisfactorily.

For the next days the column moved steadily southward, sometimes camping beside an oasis, but more often in the open. Gradually the landscape began to alter. An occasional scraggling patch of scrubland broke the monotony of the undulating sand, and an occasional bird or wild ass appeared far off in the distance. Then unexpectedly a water fowl winged across the sky before them, and Ali spurred his horse forward to tell them they would reach the Barada early the following afternoon.

When they entered the Sheik's tent for dinner that evening, he was not alone. Two of his wives sat at his feet, and numerous of his sons had gathered in the room. At first the younger boys ducked their heads and peeped at Natia, but their shyness was soon overcome by curiosity and they moved forward to sit beside her while she ate. Although the Sheik was courteous to his wives, Natia could tell that dining with strangers was a new experience for them, and that they could scarcely contain their eagerness to escape. The Sheik, however, had arranged for amusement, and although the men, down to the youngest son, enjoyed the gyrations of the group of dancing girls, his wives and Natia were more embarrassed than entertained.

Coffee and fruit juice were being served when a procession of girls entered and placed gifts before Natia and Devon. "These tokens my daughters bring express the affection we have for you," the Sheik said, then chuckled when the youngest of the little girls ran across to him and flung herself into his arms.

It was a side of the Sheik Natia had not seen before. She stared at the waist-girdle in her hands, completely bereft of speech. It was a full three inches wide, fashioned of hammered gold and studded all over with rubies and pearls. Slowly her eyes lifted to meet the Sheik's. "I will treasure it always," she said simply.

"May Allah grant you long life to enjoy it," he replied, rising to signal the end of the evening.

Devon expressed his appreciation for his own gift, cordially shook the Sheik's hand, which seemed to please him, and conducted a very dazed Natia out into the night. "I'm too excited to sleep," she said, skipping along beside him.

"You are going straight to bed," he replied, holding back the flap of their tent. "You may chatter to your heart's content once we are safe aboard the *Seahawk*. But until we are, I want you rested and alert."

"You are becoming more like a Turk every day," she gurgled, whirling about in an excess of joy. "What did the Sheik give you? I was too thrilled with my gift to notice."

"An attractive bauble," he grinned, holding out a jeweled dagger. The blade was of finest steel, but the handle aad scabbard were of solid gold and studded with emeralds interspersed with diamonds. "It will be a tale to tell our grandchildren. Now come along to bed."

Natia awakened in the night and lay for a time reliving the experiences of the past weeks. They had often been uncomfortable, and seldom far from danger, but she felt that never before had two people enjoyed a more interesting and varied wedding trip. For she had come to think of it in that way. She had loved every minute of it, but most of all she loved the pretty mare the Sheik had placed at her disposal. An idea came into her head. I will pay her one final visit, she thought, slipping from the bed without disturbing Devon.

Pausing only to don the by now bedraggled gown which had constituted her only clothing for weeks, she cautiously undid the flap of the tent and slipped outside. The camp was very quiet. Sentries were posted some distance away, their fires making bright patches in the dark, but everyone else was asleep. Locating the corral proved simple, and within a very few minutes she was able to single out the mare. She was never able to recall later exactly what happened. One minute she was rubbing her cheek against the silken nose, the next she was smothered in foul smelling robes with a hand clamped over her mouth. She struggled as best she might, but she was no match for a pair of powerful arms. Her captor strode off with her and rode away without so much as a whisper of sound that would rouse the camp.

She hoped against hope that someone would see them and set out in pursuit, but she soon abandoned the thought. Numerous half-formed ideas for escape jostled together in her mind, none of them logical enough to answer the purpose. The best thing for her to do, she decided hazily, would be to appear docile until her captors relaxed their vigil. There seemed to be quite a number of them, she surmised, and she wondered at their purpose in the camp. Stealing horses probably, she thought, and took scant comfort in the thought.

They galloped on for perhaps an hour before slowing the pace. With a start Natia realized they were passing spirits back and forth, continuing to do so until they became very drunk. Whether this augured good or ill, she couldn't know. Finally they were making little progress, and she hoped they would fall from their horses in a stupor, but she was doomed to disappointment. They still retained enough sense to truss her up with ropes when they could go no farther and stopped to sleep off the effects of drink. Soon a chorus of drunken snores broke the silence, and Natia began to struggle to free herself. A few minutes sufficed. She could not manage it. Thinking rapidly, she hit upon a plan. She would roll over and over in the sand, putting as much distance as possible between herself and them before they woke. Perhaps they would go on their way without her. What would happen to her then should Devon be unable to locate her she dared not ponder.

Every few minutes she paused to reassure herself the men still slept; the ropes chafed her wrists and sand kept getting into her mouth, but she dared not stop to rest. With an effort she forced herself up the side of a high dune and rolled down the other side, scattering a cloud of sand before her. She came to rest against a solid object which put its arms around her and fastened its lips on hers. "Colin!" she whispered, blinking the dust from her eyes.

"Know my kiss in the dark, do you?" he chuckled softly, while cutting the ropes binding her. "We will go into that later. For now, let's get the hell out of here."

His horse was tethered a short distance away, but sound carries far in the desert so he waited until they had covered several miles before breaking into a gallop. He held her cradled in his arms, her head resting on his shoulder. "I am almost afraid to ask," he remarked, looking down into her face.

"You want to know how I got myself into this predicament."

"Something like that."

"I went to say goodbye to the mare. How did you find me?"

"I have been following you almost from the beginning. There was little I could do but trail along and wait."

"Colin, I thought Muslims didn't drink."

"The faithful don't. Fortunately, my little adventuress, there is little of the religious in your erstwhile companions."

"I seem to be forever in a coil."

"At least you have the sense to help yourself."

"When did you first miss me?"

"It seems I am no longer able to sleep unless soft curves press against me." Chuckling, he slipped his fingers beneath her gown, his kisses growing passionate as he fondled her familiar body with warm hands. He let the reins drop over the horse's neck, and its headlong pace subsided into a gentle canter. Lifting her up, he placed her astride his lap facing him and lowered her onto his throbbing manhood. She clung to him, returning his kisses with an ardor to match his own, as the motion of the cantering horse brought them pleasure so exquisite they were left trembling in its aftermath. They had no need for words, and rode back to the camp content to clasp each other close.

CHAPTER NINE

They rode in under the shadow of their tent out of sight of the sentries on guard. Devon swung down, still holding her in his arms, and set her on her feet. "Try not to fret," he said, bending to kiss her on the cheek. "I shan't be long. The Sheik will soon have his prisoners."

"I know that drunken men are incapable of mounting a defense," she snapped, worry eating at her heart. "Must you treat me like a child?"

"Good!" he chuckled. "Your tongue remains razor sharp. You have suffered little from your plight."

She smiled, but with a touch of restraint. "Please do not heed me," she murmured, looking away. "The Sheik will need you to guide his forces. You should have capital sport."

He said, concern in his voice, "Dearest, I have no notion of distressing you, but I must go. You do see that, don't you?"

"You must think me very foolish."

"Yes," he replied, in a rallying tone. "I rather fancy I do. There is no cause for alarm. Preserve your dignity, my love, and go to bed."

She giggled suddenly. "After the way you have just

used me, you are hardly one to speak of dignity," she gurgled, and went within on the words.

Although she was very tired from the stresses she had undergone, she could not think of retiring until Devon was safely restored to her. So she sat down to wait, the sounds of the tribesmen gathering for battle clearly audible. It was the same in every tent, she knew; woman always waited, sick with apprehension, for her man's return. For the next three hours she scarcely stirred from her chair. One of the Sheik's wives sent around a slave with fruit juice and little cakes, but other than the one interruption, she endured the suspense alone. And then finally, when her nerves were stretched to breaking, she heard the jingle of harness, followed a moment later by the confused murmur of voices outside the tent.

Running to the open flap, she peered out into the dark. "Is that you, Colin?" she cried. "Oh, I am so thankful! Come in at once!"

"I am in no fit state to enter," he replied in a tired but cheerful voice. "Just bring me a basin of water—"

"What does that signify, pray?" she exclaimed, then gasped upon catching sight of him. His robe was filthy, his hair disheveled, and one sleeve was torn and spattered with blood. "You are hurt!" she added quickly.

"It is not my gore," he explained, coming in. "I am only worn out and hungry. Be a good girl and find me something to eat while I wash. My appearance must be appalling."

"It is," she agreed. "Well, never mind. Just get out of that horrible clothing while I forage around the camp. Someone is always cooking something," she added, hurrying from the room.

By the time she returned with kebobs still hot from the fire and a chunk of crusty bread, he had stripped and washed and was waiting with a sheet wrapped around his middle. A weary frown creased his brow, and his eyes were heavy and bloodshot. "I can't remember when I have been more tired," he remarked, tearing off a piece of bread. "The blackguards may have been three parts drunk, but they fought like men possessed."

"Were any of the tribesmen injured?"

"A scratch or two; nothing to signify. We had the advantage of surprise. I almost felt sorry for the brigands, poor devils."

Her eyes grew round. "Weren't they taken as prisoners?" she asked.

"Not a one," he replied, his mouth full of lamb. "Life is cheap here, my dear, and the provocation was great. But it is probably for the best. A quick death beats the Sultan's tender mercy any way you look at it."

"And what was your role in this tawdry affair?"

"Mine? Oh, I did my part, you may be sure of that. If it had not been for the Sheik's orders, I daresay I would have accounted for some few more of the devils."

"I see," she said. "The Sheik wanted you safely out of it, so naturally you immediately flung yourself into the thick of it."

He regarded her with a grim little smile. "You would not have me a coward, Natia."

"Certainly not," she agreed with irony. "You would admit that all this waiting around not knowing whether you were alive or dead could not possibly age me before my time."

"Taking the mare back to England with you should restore your youth," he remarked, grinning. "The spoils of war, my dear, from a grateful Sheik. He values your part in this unholy affair only slightly below my own. My stallion, I might add, goes with us also. Which reminds me. He is sending us on ahead tomorrow. The tribe will tarry here until its wounds have healed."

Neither the danger he had been in nor the ease with which he brushed it aside could be expected to please her, but when they presently went back to bed she felt that things might have turned out much worse and held her tongue.

They set out early the next morning with a sizeable escort as swiftly as the horses could carry them. The farther they rode the more mountainous the country-side became, with high-peaked hills and gushing streams. Finally, shortly before noon, Ali led them into a wood beside the river Barada where they soon came upon a bubbling spring. "We will wait here, my lord," he said, indicating the mossy ground.

"Shouldn't you return to camp?" Devon asked. "The *Seahawk* won't drop anchor until after dark."

"Brigands often camp in these hills," Ali explained, shaking his head. "Our Sheik sent us to protect you in case of attack, though it seems unlikely they will have seen us upon the road. It is their custom to sleep until the sun rides high."

"I wondered why we did not time our arrival to coincide with that of my ship."

"The hand of Allah guides our Sheik, my lord," Ali replied with a confidence Devon would have been much relieved to share.

Natia sat down upon the ground and patted the mossy earth for him to sit down beside her. It was not such a conclusion to their adventure as she had imagined. Could it be, she wondered, that after all the danger and intrigue, they would simply stroll aboard the *Seahawk* as if setting forth on a Sunday cruise? It seemed, incredibly, that that was exactly what they were about to do.

"I must own we can be more comfortable now that

the time to embark is here, but somehow I hate to leave this land," she said, glancing at the friendly tribesmen with their dark eyes and flashing smiles.

"Yes, my love, and so do I," Devon replied, turning on his back to lie with his head in her lap.

"Only fancy," she mused, idly tracing a finger about his lips. "Nurse will shortly be scolding me and talking of the consequences due my station—as though I cannot be trusted to act as I ought."

"I think you need have no fear of that," he murmured, kissing the tips of her fingers. "She will be too relieved at seeing you to ring a peal over your head. She will more probably drench you with her tears."

In this he was woefully wrong, as they were to discover. All that Nurse had endured had not changed her one whit, as became apparent the instant they climbed aboard the *Seahawk.*

Before that was to take place, however, they were forced to endure additional moments of suspense. As the afternoon progressed, Devon began to feel almost benign. To have secured Natia's safety pleased him much more than the satisfaction he felt at having outwitted the Sultan's men so neatly. He smiled to think of the possibilities thus called up. That he was not as yet destined to live out his days in peace with a wife and children by his side never occurred to him; he was not one to gaze with dire forebodings upon the future, and as such folly was beyond his comprehension, it was not to be supposed that he might question the idea of their continued safety once they were beyond the boundaries of the Sultan's domain.

Almost upon the dusk the sound of horses pounding by upon the road below echoed through the wood. Ali frowned and moved quietly in and out among the trees until the road was within his view. Surprised to see a large party of brigands heading for a hill just beyond their own, he turned and doubled back, signaling for silence until all sounds of the horsemen had died away in the distance.

"We will go now, lordship," he said to Devon. "The offal gather in large numbers. Why, I do not know. We will find it safer on the banks of the Barada."

"Come, Natia," Devon said, helping her up, a cold fear clutching at his heart. "Ali, you must leave us now. Escape with your men while you can."

"We will not run away, lordship," Ali objected.

But Devon paid him no heed, insisting that he and Natia would attract less attention if alone. Their farewells were brief and from the heart; Devon then led Natia off through the trees, always keeping out of sight in the shadows, until they came to the road. She would have immediately dashed across, but he laid a restraining hand upon her arm and stood listening intently until in the distance he heard a brigand laugh. There was no help for it; they must expose themselves to gain cover on the other side. And so, with a silent prayer upon their lips, they stole across the moon-washed road and did not pause until they found haven among the reeds on the river bank.

The night drew darker by degrees as clouds formed overhead, obscuring the moon. Natia, held close in the circle of Devon's arms, felt no fear, but he knew their hiding place could be discovered at any moment and strained his eyes for that first welcome glimpse of the *Seahawk*. It seemed they waited an eternity, but at last the yacht's shadowy bulk loomed up before them in the dark, and they swam out to meet the boat dispatched to pick them up. Natia was by now looking upon their escapade as one more adventure added to the list, even to the point of finding the experience of being handed up the side of the *Seahawk* into the grasp of a waiting sailor to be great fun.

They had no more than set foot on deck than Nurse bustled forward and fixed Natia with a stern eye. "You will catch your death out in this damp air,

Missy," she said, putting an arm about Natia's shoulders. "Come inside at once!"

"Nettle!" Natia cried. "Aren't you glad to see me?"

Nurse sniffed. "That's as may be," she said tartly, "but you could take a chill. It's out of that heathenish garb and into a hot tub for you, make no mistake about it."

For the first time since they had left the shadows of the river bank for those final hazardous minutes to the yacht, Devon's laugh rang out. "Run along," he instructed Natia. "I told you she would rejoice to see you."

The desire to remain on deck with him, and yearnings for the luxury of a tub, warred within her breast. At last opting for the bath, she followed Nurse to the master suite with a bathroom opening out of it. The salon's walls were painted white, and deep chairs upholstered in blue damask stood about the room. A large bed draped in clouds of cotton voile was just visible through the partially opened bedroom door. "You look a fright," came Nurse's comment the instant the door to the salon closed behind them.

Natia whirled on her. "Of course I look a fright!" she cried, about at the end of her tether. "We have spent weeks eluding the Sultan's Janissaries under the most primitive conditions imaginable, and all you can find to do is to comment on my appearance! I daresay you looked little better yourself when you first came aboard!"

A slow smile spread across Nurse's face. "So," she said. "It's a lusty land, Missy. Are you happy?"

In spite of herself, Natia chuckled. "Go draw my bath, you wretched gossip, before I box your ears."

"His lordship deserves a loving wife," Nurse declared, standing her ground. "I intend to see he gets one."

Natia flushed slightly. "Go order something decent for him to eat and then come back to help me," she said, disrobing and handing over her bedraggled gown. "Just get rid of it, I don't care how," she added, going into the bathroom to draw her bath.

Alone, she luxuriated in the steaming tub, lathering herself with the flower-scented soap and scrubbing all over with the soft cloth. Suddenly a draft touched her wet skin, and she turned her head just as Devon stepped in to join her. "Move over, sweet," he said. "The tub will hold the two of us."

Giggling, she sank down until the water hid her breasts. "By the beard of the Prophet," she said outrageously, "is a lady to have no privacy?"

Reaching out, he pulled her unresisting body into his arms and ran his hands over her slippery flesh. "Fine talk for a peeress," he chuckled, cupping her breasts to tease the nipples with his thumbs. "Methinks we will become so clean we will fair wash our skin away."

Laughing, she squirmed out of his grasp. "Methinks you had best be about it before the water cools," she said, holding out the soap.

She thought him bested, but the next instant she found herself snatched against his chest. Bending his head, his mouth sought hers and took fierce possession of her lips.

Oblivious to everything around them, they remained unaware of Nurse's approach until she walked into the room. She stopped dead in midstride, the expostulation she was about to utter dying stillborn on her tongue. Devon flushed to the roots of his hair, but Natia only seemed amused.

Nurse, quickly recovering, said rather brusquely: "It's time to get out of there, Missy. You will wrinkle your skin like a prune."

Natia, well beyond the power of speech, could only shake with suppressed laughter within the shelter of Devon's arms.

"You need not stay!" he snapped at Nurse. "I will see to her ladyship."

"I laid out a warm nightgown on the bed. See she puts it on."

"Good God, woman! Will you get out of here?"

"Lord, sir, you needn't mind me," Nurse assured him. "I diapered Missy almost from the day she was born."

Devon glared. "That may be, but you didn't diaper me!"

Nurse went towards the door, then turned her head to look at him. "If she doesn't behave like a proper wife to your lordship, you just let me know," she said and left, closing the door behind her.

Devon muttered something unintelligible under his breath and turned his gaze upon the unrepentant bit of fluff collapsed in glee across his chest. He set his teeth. "It isn't funny," he gritted.

Natia went off on a peal of laughter. "If you could have seen your face!" she gurgled, looping her arms about his neck.

His eyes were very close to hers. "I want you to listen carefully," he began, his gaze locked with hers. "I will not be made to look the fool by servants in my own home. Call it my damnable pride, or call it what you will, you will resign yourself to the fact that your old Nurse won't have access to our quarters. She will come when sent for and depart when told to do so. I mean this, Natia. No woman but you is privileged to look upon my private parts."

"I—don't think she—saw—"

"What is intimate between us is sacred. Do you think I will permit anyone to share it?"

"No, nor will I," she replied, rising in some confusion and stepping from the tub.

"Come back here!" he demanded softly, holding out his hand.

"The water grows cold," she temporized, evading his grasp and wrapping a towel about herself.

He bounded from the tub dripping wet and was on her in two strides. "Don't imagine I don't intend making love to you tonight," he said, scooping her up in his arms and carrying her to the bed. "I have thought of little else all day," he admitted, snatching away the towel.

"You have only minutes ago read me a lecture on modesty," she shot back, reaching out to draw the cover over herself.

He stayed her hand. "Before the servants, sweet. Not us. You have nothing to hide I haven't seen many times before. God, but you're a pretty sight," he murmured, his eyes sweeping over her. "When I get you back to England, I will need to hide you from the world."

She began to laugh. "And what will you be doing in the meantime? I will wager you are acquainted with every lady between Devon Hall and London. Well, sir, in the future you may look all you like, but you are not to touch."

"Am I not, indeed? Nonsensical girl. Why should I wish to? You are wholly adorable."

"No, I'm not," she protested, smiling saucily up at him. "I am as disagreeable as you are, Colin Fortas Devereau, and you know it."

"If it will please you, I will engage to quarrel with you every morning before breakfast."

She eyed him askance. "You talk much, but you aren't saying much!" she declared.

"On the contrary, I am saying everything that is civil."

"Yes, you are, and none of it to the point."

Chuckling, he tumbled her back against the pillows. "Your tongue is a never-ending source of delight to me, my sweet," he said, moving up and over her, "but I'll hear no more from it this night."

When Natia woke the following morning, she found him already risen and dressed "Go back to sleep, sweetheart," he said. "It's early."

"No," she said, reaching for a robe. "I want to go on deck. Have you breakfasted?"

"Marston has just this minute brought it," he replied, going with her into the salon. "A lighter put out from an island during the night with dispatches from home. The news is bad, I'm afraid."

"In what way?" she asked, taking the chair he held for her.

"Napoleon has succeeded in amassing an army of colossal size. Even Marshal Ney has joined him."

"Well, it is our own fault, I suppose. Someone should have seen to it that he didn't escape from exile to return and stir up more trouble. I should think the French wouldn't want him back. They should have learned their lesson," she added, passing him his cup.

"Thank you, my dear. No, it seems they haven't, though it is understandable from their point of view. They yearn for a return to their days of glory, and King Louis has proven to be abysmally inept. He has, in fact, fled with his court to Ghent, leaving all of France to flock to Napoleon's banner."

"Then war is certain? I should think the countries of Europe would band together to meet the threat."

"They have, but if we can believe the dispatches, it is an uneasy alliance at best. Everyone from the Prince of Orange to some Prussian general—I forget his name—seems to think himself capable of leading the Allied armies. Wellington will have his hands full."

"How so? Is he not the Field Marshal?"

"He is, but he must come to grips with the incredibly inflated egos of minor princelings and high-ranking officers who seem to have more hair than wit. The Duke has displayed fine tact in establishing his headquarters in Brussels."

Natia grasped the significance of this at once and cast him a shrewd look. "If you are thinking to abandon me at Devon Hall while you take up residence in Brussels, thank you, no."

He was in the act of conveying a bite of egg to his mouth and paused with the fork suspended in mid-air. "You frighten me at times," he said. "Must you read my every thought?"

"You know me too well to suppose I will let you go without me. You are thinking of the danger. Stuff and nonsense! After what we have been through, it cannot signify."

He laughed. "That is where you are out, my dear. England is, after all, just across the Channel. If Brussels should become unsafe, we could always go home. I was thinking you might find it boring. I go on business, sweet."

"You can be so very odious at times," she declared, rather startled. "It seems extraordinary that you must speak in riddles."

"I own extensive properties in France inherited from my maternal grandmother. So you see, my dear, we have a considerable stake in the outcome of this war."

"I thought the French confiscated all properties during their revolution."

"They did, but mine were restored to me by Louis the Eighteenth after he became King. Before you comment, yes, I have every intention of disposing of them at the earliest opportunity."

She wrinkled her brow. "Colin, whatever will I wear."

"So speaks the eternal woman," he chuckled. "You will be pleased to know that among the orders I have dispatched to my man of business, one concerns you. In addition to a house he is to rent for us in Brussels, he is to engage the services of the finest dressmaker the city has to offer."

"Beast!" she smiled. "You intended taking me all along."

"That is just what I was about to comment, my dear."

"I own, now I think about it, that I hope we will not find Brussels thin of society due to this odious war."

"To be sure, my love, so do I."

"I will need the services of a coiffeur, Colin. My hair is a fright. Will you just look at it!"

"Must I?" he said, the devil in his shining eyes. "All during breakfast I have been at considerable pains not to do so."

"I'm quite sure," she said, putting down her napkin, "that there was never so provoking a person as you!"

"Don't disturb yourself, my love. Only recollect that last evening I told you I would engage to quarrel with you at breakfast if it would make you happy."

It was too absurd. She could not help but laugh. "I only wish I could think of something sufficiently cutting to put you in your place," she remarked, rising.

He smiled at her and took her chin in his hand to turn her face up to his. "Poor darling. Can you not?" he said, kissing her deeply.

She returned his embrace with great willingness, then said, indicating the garment she was wearing, "After living in one gown for weeks, I would hate to think this robe will be it until we reach Brussels."

"It is called a caftan, my precious simpleton," he told her tenderly. "Marston unearthed a number of them for you, I have no idea where. It looks comfortable."

"It is," she admitted, glancing down in some doubt at the loose silk garment which hung free from her shoulders to the floor. "What is our first port of call?"

"I have no notion. The nearest to Brussels, I expect."

"Surely you jest!"

"Not at all. If you wish to visit some area of the Mediterranean, we will do so after the war."

"But this is abominable! Where am I to shop?"

"My dear, you look lovely. I will regret seeing my brave little houri turn back into a sedate English gentlewoman. Besides, Napoleon's soldiers control the coasts of France. There is no place you can shop."

"Oh!" she said, disappointed. "You must think me silly."

"Very silly," he agreed, kissing her again. "I am still too delighted with you to object."

She said no more, but she was not ill-pleased. "Let us go on deck. I have a yearning to feel the breeze against my face."

It was a fine clear morning, though a trifle warm. Riafat came up to them where they stood beside the ship's railing, and bowed. "Welcome, ladyship," he said, salaaming. "Allah has seen fit to smile upon you."

"Thank you, Riafat. I am beginning to think he has. So you go with us?"

"Of a certainty, ladyship. I have no desire to trade servitude to the Sultan for slavery under the French." Turning to Devon, he bowed. "I have taken charge of the Arabians, lordship. Your English sailors seem not to know one end of a horse from the other."

"When we arrive in Brussels, I plan to make you bodyguard to her ladyship. I wouldn't trust her safety to anyone but you."

"Really, Colin!" Natia exclaimed. "I certainly have no objection to Riafat's company, but that is doing it rather brown."

"It is not all colorful uniforms and regimental insignia, my dear. Riffraff batten on the fringes of any army; this one is drawn from many nations, don't forget. There is no telling what will follow in its wake."

"Oh!" she said. "Is that a bad thing, do you think?"

"The worst!" he replied.

She thought this over, then said, "I don't expect to come in contact with undesirable persons. I'm sure I shall feel perfectly at ease."

Upon their arrival in Brussels some weeks later, however, her confidence in her ability to see to herself underwent a shock. The city was crowded to overflowing: housing was at a premium, with soldiers billeted in many homes, and the hotels were booked to capacity; contingents of troops under many banners marched through the streets and an occasional piece of artillery rumbled over the cobblestones; officers and their ladies strolled in the great Place Royale and common soldiers swaggered through the streets, some of them with harlots on their arms.

As their carriage drew nearer to the house they would occupy in the Rue Ducale, Devon's coachman was obliged to slow the horses to a walk, and Natia, leaning forward in the seat, was surprised to see numerous conveyances with a crest emblazoned upon their doors. It would seem, she thought, that Brussels was the place to be, at least for the present. She was no less surprised when they drew up before an imposing residence and Devon stepped down onto the paved courtyard and turned to hold out his hand to her. The house was built of stone and brick, with shuttered windows, and with the coach house and stable around at the back.

Lord Sherwood came through the front door just as Natia placed her hand on Devon's arm to go inside. He looked rather harried, but neither his eyes nor his smile held any hint of the frustration he had felt over his mother-in-law's attitude toward Natia on the occasion of their earlier acquaintance. "We have been expecting you this age," he said, hurrying forward to wring Devon's hand. "I was beginning to think some evil had befallen you upon the road."

"No, we are quite safe," Devon replied, surveying his brother-in-law from under raised brows. "I had not known that you were here. Mama, too?"

"Well, yes," Thomas admitted, not quite able to meet his eyes.

"Dear me," remarked Devon.

Thomas turned to Natia. "I had forgotten how pretty you are, my dear," he smiled. "But do not let us be standing about out here. You must be chilled, and we have a roaring fire inside."

They found Lorinda and the Dowager Lady Devon established in the drawing room. Thomas drew Natia to a chair before the fire, procured a glass of Madeira for her, and stationed himself by her side for all the world like a faithful spaniel ready to defend his mistress. His worst fears proved groundless.

The Dowager Lady Devon broached the subject uppermost in all their minds immediately the obeisances were concluded. "I don't doubt you wonder at our being here," she said, her eyes on Natia. "If you find you cannot tolerate our presence in your home, I would not blame you. I have lately been finding it difficult to live with myself."

Natia could not help looking astounded. She had thought that after their earlier acquaintance at Devon Hall, the breech was far too wide to mend. She could not like having his family take up residence with them under the circumstances, but she was persuaded Devon would feel hurt and embarrassed if his mother were forced to put up at a hotel when he was in possession of a house sufficient to shelter them all. A high color was in her cheeks, but good breeding compelled her to say, "You are not to think it. We shall do all within our power to make your stay comfortable."

"Thank you. If I could, I would undo the mischief my conduct brought upon you. Since my husband's death, I have been answerable to no one but myself. I became unprincipled, a Grand Dame without compunction. I can only beg your forgiveness."

"I do forgive you," Natia assured her, considerably moved. "The circumstances of our marriage made it particularly trying for you. In the circles in which you have always moved, one's every action is remarked and gossiped about. It is the same in Russia. To be held up to ridicule by one's friends—"

"No!" the Dowager interrupted. "You are not to take the blame upon yourself. During these weeks when we have not known whether we would ever see the two of you again, I have had ample time for reflection. Don't make excuses for me, child. Through my own misdeeds, I came close to losing that which I hold most dear."

"We will forget the unpleasantness and start again. People have short memories. Some new scandal always comes along to claim their notice."

"There will be no scandal, Natia. May I call you that? Thank you. Well, Natia, at least I had the good sense to publicly applaud the match. We have put it about that we are in Brussels to await your return from your honeymoon. No one will be the wiser."

Tea was announced at this moment, and soon they were gathered around the table in the dining room partaking of cold sliced beef and scalloped oysters. Unable to contain himself, Thomas put forth a tentative query concerning their adventures, then listened with rapt attention to Devon's highly censored recitation of their progress across Turkey. Natia, intrigued, found it difficult to relate to the ladylike amblings through the Sultan's domain falling so glibly from his tongue. The meal at an end, she proposed going upstairs to rest, but Devon, after raising her fingers to his lips, a very tender expression in his eyes, went out in search of news.

She was seated at her dressing table when he entered her room some two hours later. He had already changed to evening dress and carried a parcel in his hand. "You look lovely," he murmured, dropping the package in her lap and bending over to plant a kiss on her nape.

"I will rather hate giving up my caftans," she replied, glancing down at the silk garment embroidered on the sleeves and down the front with torquoise, seed pearls, and gold thread.

"Nonsense," he said, taking a chair facing her. "There is no reason for you to give them up."

"You spin a fascinating tale, my lord, but there is aught to gain my raising eyebrows."

"You will wear them to please me in the privacy of our home," he returned, leaning back at ease. "I have no wish to forget moon-filled nights passed with a desert houri in my arms. Open your present."

"Is there some special reason?" she said, undoing the ribbon.

"You deserve a treat."

Natia lifted out a slender chain with a gold medallion incised with the profile of the Duke of Wellington suspended from it. "Thank you," she murmured, fastening it about her throat.

"No," he said. "It is my place to thank you for not turning my mother away from our door."

"Very handsomely put. Your opinion of me must be sad indeed."

"It could not be higher, as you very well know, but you can see what an anxious position I was in. With all her faults, she is my mother. Still, you have only to say the word—"

She cast him a shrewd look. "I know you a little

too well to accept that offer. You would be miserable. What news of the war were you able to glean?"

"There seems to be a great deal of tension in the town, but whether we are to believe the gossip in the coffee houses, I couldn't say. Rumor has it that the German generals are fighting among themselves over who will lead them, and the Saxons are in an uproar over an oath of allegiance to the King of Prussia. Even the Peace party at home is sniping from the sidelines."

"How can we possibly defeat Napoleon if we continually quarrel among ourselves?"

"A good question, my dear. We must just trust in Wellington to pull his rag-tag army together."

CHAPTER TEN

Much to Natia's delight, the dressmaker turned out to be a much-sought-after French couturière. Before the revolution the aristocracy had been regular customers of her Paris shop; she had been wise enough to know herself suspect for no other reason than this, and had had the good sense to flee before the guillotine could caress her slender neck. During these days Devon was seldom to be found at home. Manlike, he fled from the premises the moment Madame Esteray arrived each morning with her attendant assistants, until he judged the invasion over for the day. On his orders, nothing was left undone. Gradually the rows of gowns in Natia's wardrobe grew until even Nurse became satisfied with their numbers.

The gaieties of Brussels continued unabated. Everyone seemed bent on pleasure-seeking as if in fear the outcome of the war would put a period to their happiness. By throwing oneself into an endless round of routs and balls one could forget one's dread. As for the Bruxellois, gold flowed freely into their pockets, so they welcomed the visitors with open arms.

Scarcely an evening passed that Devon did not relate the circumstances of having come upon a friend from home. The coffee houses and clubs that dotted the city became gathering places where gentlemen met to gamble and exchange news on the progress of the army. No bit of information on the military situation received second-hand was too extravagant to be repeated, no piece of folly sufficiently shocking to set the town by its ears. Everyone seemed determined to prove the truth of everything that was said, regardless of how ridiculous the assertion. Devon listened to it all, but put little stock in any of it. Wellington's energy and capacity for detail were well known; the man was incapable of anticipating defeat at Napoleon's hands. He was an extraordinary fellow, a commander whose ability had been amply proven. Devon saw no cause for alarm.

Natia learned at breakfast one morning that they would attend a fete that evening given by the Duke in honor of King William as a sop for English troops having been employed on garrison duty instead of the Prussians. She would have preferred receiving the invitation days before, but in wartime the usual courtesies went by the board. Naturally she needed the entire day to dress, and when she descended the staircase Devon knew the time had been well spent. She was a vision in turquoise satin which clung enticingly to her slender form, but she could not help feeling conscious of the diamonds in her hair and about her throat.

"Your mother insisted I wear them," she explained defensively.

"Of course," he said. "I made no remark."

"She said they are part of the Devon collection."

"They are."

She cast him a questioning glance. "They are so—large."

He smiled, but said nothing, and escorted her out front to the waiting carriage. "You are accustomed to adventure," he murmured, handing her into her seat. "I hope it will not prove an insipid evening."

She avoided his teasing gaze; but when he had settled down beside her and the carriage moved forward, she said: "Who do you suppose will be present?"

"All the world, I should think. A number of my friends are anxious to accord you their flattering attention. I assume I will find it difficult to secure a dance with you."

It seemed he was correct on all counts. When they arrived the salons were already crowded, very much too warm, and a kaleidoscope of color. Life Guardsmen in scarlet and gold rubbed shoulders with the Dutch in blue and Belgian dragoons in rifle-green. Guests who preferred less strenuous exercise to the ballroom floor stood about in little groups discussing the war and listened with rapt attention to any soldier who could be induced to join them. Natia was aware that many pairs of eyes were fixed upon her as she moved through the throng on Devon's arm, but she did not betray that she was aware of the scrutiny by so much as the flicker of an eyelid. Their progress was necessarily slow, with Devon pausing to introduce her to friends before guiding her onward toward the ballroom. The orchestra had just struck up a waltz and he led her onto the floor, remarking that he would have one dance at least before someone came along to claim her. As they glided about the room Natia could not help but note that smiles seemed artificial and forced. It was as if gaiety could banish all worry.

Her reflections were interrupted by the Duke of Wellington coming in with King William at his side. The music died away and the dancing came to a halt as the soldiers stood rigidly at attention, the gentlemen bowed deeply, and the ladies sank to the floor in graceful curtsies. The Duke, a master of diplomacy when not confronted with exasperating problems of the army, had done everything he could to bolster the ego of his guest of honor. His party included an impressing array of faces, among them the British Ambassador, numerous Generals, and the Duke's aides-de-camp. Since—as was usual at social gatherings—the majority of the people present were known to the Duke, and his memory for names was phenomenal, their progress around the floor went smoothly. The ballroom traversed, he then escorted King William from the room, and the orchestra struck up the waltz again.

Devon slipped his arm about Natia's waist to continue the dance, but a hand grasped him on the shoulder. "My dance, old boy," a voice spoke in his ear, causing him to turn his head.

"Drake!" Devon ejaculated, gripping the hand held out to him. "When did you arrive in town?"

"Just this morning. Are you going to present me to your bride? You must, you know. I insist."

"Natia—the Earl of Ardley. Drake is happily married, my dear. Otherwise I wouldn't make the introduction."

Natia sketched a curtsy and then looked up to find a pair of cool gray eyes surveying her. They held a great deal of lively appreciation in their depths, and a smile curved the Earl's lips. "How do you do!" she smiled in return, extending her hand.

The Earl took it in his and bent his head to kiss it. "I trust you will grant me what is left of this waltz," he said, amusement quivering in his voice.

"He has no heart," Devon remarked. "My dear, send him about his business."

"Go entertain Annette," the Earl chuckled in reply. "You will find her in the salon."

Natia instinctively knew them close as brothers, sharing a friendship that went back many years. "Yes, Colin, do run along." She smiled and laid her hand upon the Earl's shoulder.

He danced beautifully, dipping and swaying about

the room with her. Neither spoke for several minutes, but presently Natia raised her eyes to his face. "What brought you to Brussels?" she inquired pleasantly.

He smiled down at her. "A cousin of mine is stationed nearby with Sir Vivian's Hussars. Nothing would do but for the family to gather. Paul is a bit embarrassed to have us here, I know. What brings you and Colin to Brussels?"

"Business, or so he says. Personally I think he enjoys being in the thick of things."

"Yes, so do we all. My wife tells me we remind her of little boys playing at soldier. I expect most of us would be about as much use to Wellington as Caroline Lamb's spaniel pup."

At that Natia's enchanting gurgle of laughter escaped her. "I heard the animal nipped General Maitland on a finger."

"It doesn't seem the least singular to me. If I were the pup, I am sure I wouldn't relish being plucked from the charmer's lap."

"Lady Caroline has a very unsettling effect, from what I can discover," she remarked, amusement in her tone. "She quite puts the rest of us in the shade."

"She is lovely, I will grant you that. But you aren't eclipsed by her beauty, nor is my wife."

"Oh?" she said. "Are your compliments ever commonplace?"

"No, I meant it. But come see for yourself. Annette is just through this door."

The fell in with the stream of dancers quitting the floor for the cooler air of the salon, and entered the large, brilliantly lit room to find it already full of people. Devon was located at a table against the wall in company with a group of strangers.

"Here you are, my dear," he said, rising. "Annette has been waiting to meet you. The Countess of Ardley—Lady Devon."

Natia found herself enfolded in a perfumed embrace, her mind in a whirl. Lady Ardley was no longer in the first flush of her youth. She was twenty-six years of age and the mother of two hopeful off-spring, a boy not quite seven and a daughter just turned three. If anything, motherhood had only heightened her beauty. Her figure remained trim, and her skin retained its youthful bloom. In a twinkling Natia was seated beside her, acknowledging the introduction to others in the party. The elderly lady in blue sarcenet and a turban towering above improbably yellow hair turned out to be Lady Hart-ford, Ardley's aunt, a woman much given to abrupt speech. Natia smiled into a pair of surprisingly bright eyes, agreed to name her Aunt Agatha, and liked her on sight. She felt equally drawn to Sir Carlton and Lady Ellen Bellamy. When compared with Sir Carl-ton's tall thinness, Lady Ellen appeared fragile and helpless indeed. But Natia was not misled. Lady Ellen had only to flutter her lashes and smile appealingly for him to become putty in her hands. Paul, Lord Wrexly, son of Lady Ellen by a former marriage, and the final member of the party, was discovered to be the cousin of whom the Earl had spoken. Handsome in scarlet and gold regimentals, and with a ready wit and easy smile, Natia thought him the most engaging rattlebox she had yet to meet.

"Devon, this is piracy," he grinned, expropriating the chair next to Natia's. "I should send my seconds to call on you. With this town woefully short of beauties, it was confoundedly underhanded of you to have married Natia."

"I will allow that to be true," Devon replied bland-ly, taking a chair, perforce, across the table from her.

"Be quiet, you foolish boy," Agatha intervened. "You will put Natia to the blush."

"Not a bit of it," Natia gurgled. "I will help him locate a charmer."

"What of Lady Grenville?" Drake remarked, surveying Paul from beneath lowered lids. "Her family is an old one, remember, and perfectly respectable."

It was a long-standing joke between them, and one they both enjoyed. "Only recollect the evils of the situation," Paul shot back, chuckling. "It's a little vulgar to speak of it—well, very vulgar if you must—but she no doubt has a stammer."

. "That certainly is a consideration," Drake agreed.

"I should rather think it is. Tell me, Natia," he said, turning twinkling eyes on her. "Do you think it fair to throw a lady at my head?"

"Not if she stammers. Does she?"

"Lord, I don't know. I've never met the chit. It is Aunt Agatha's idea, you understand. But I shouldn't own myself surprised to find she does. Granddaughters of girlhood friends usually do."

"Heartless boy," Agatha said with perfect composure. "It may interest you to know she will be in attendance here tonight."

"Don't say so!" Paul gasped, stunned. "You never arranged for us to meet?"

. "I did, but don't alarm yourself. I see she has just come in, but if you find an introduction abhorrent, I shan't press you."

"I should rather think I do," he replied, following the direction of her glance. "Good God!" he added blankly, staring in stupefaction at the ravishing creature approaching in company with her mother.

The next instant he was on his feet, his gaze fastened on flaming red hair glowing in the candlelight and the greenest eyes he had ever seen. In his bemused state, she seemed to him to glide across the intervening space between them. Her mother reached the table first, and by the time the civilities had been exchanged he had recovered sufficiently to charm Lady Grenville into accompanying him to the ballroom floor. Sir Carlton and Lady Ellen soon followed, and the elderly ladies went to visit at the table of mutual friends, leaving the Devons and the Ardleys alone together.

"Paul will be out of all conceit with himself," Drake remarked, chuckling. "He has been resisting the acquaintance of Lady Grenville for some time. Our stay here should prove more interesting than I first thought."

"Pray, don't suggest such a thing," Annette implored, grimacing. "I could not bear his thinking himself in love again. He is always in such raptures over his latest flirt."

"One day he will settle down," Drake assured her. "Colin did; Lord knows he played the field."

"He did?" Natia said instantly, much intrigued. "Tell me about it."

"Don't give them an opportunity to brag," Annette implored, laughing. "When you have been married as long as I have, Natia, you will realize they will go to any lengths before they run their course."

"Well, Colin?" Natia said, looking arch. "I daresay you have something to say?"

"I?" he said. "Nothing at all, my dear."

"Then I must rely on Annette to learn your secrets. You will come to call?" she added, smiling upon her new-found friend.

"Tomorrow, if I may. I own, now I've met you, that Brussels will prove most spritely. I was so afraid I would hear little other than talk of the war from one day to the next. Do you ride?"

"Yes, at every opportunity. I have my Arabian mare with me. She is such a dear."

"An Arabian!" Annette gasped, astounded. "Wherever did you get her?"

"She was given to me by—" Natia, pausing, glanced at Devon, "—a friend," she finished somewhat lamely.

Devon, who had his eyes on her, interposed to turn the conversation toward less dangerous channels. He was assisted readily enough by Drake, who privately entertained the notion there was something Devon did not wish revealed, and for the remainder of the time they spent together nothing was discussed but social topics.

Natia expressed her liking for the Ardleys during the drive home. "I only hope I look half so well after having babies," she concluded on a wistful note.

"You will, my dear. Annette had a disagreeable experience while carrying their eldest, but she weathered it in style. One can only wonder at the resilience of women."

"I have had something of the sort myself, you will recall, and I can tell you it was sometimes a very disagreeable experience. Or have you forgotten?"

"Certainly not. It was not very easy on me at times, but that you found it less than high adventure comes as news to me."

She gave her enchanting gurgle of laughter and said, "Do but recollect, I beg you. At your hands I learned things I am quite sure no gently nurtured female should ever know."

"Very true," he said, putting his arm about her shoulders.

"How abominable of you to say so," she teased, subsiding against his chest. "You have turned me into a wanton."

"I like you that way, my love. Did you know?"

"Of course," she chortled, turning her face up to receive his kiss. "I'll wager Annette's experience could never rival mine."

"In some ways her experience resembles yours, my dear. She was kidnapped by spies and sold to a smuggler who held her in France for ransom. Her son, Redding, was born there."

"Since he is not quite seven, this must have occurred before Napoleon was banished to Elba," Natia mused. "How very terrifying it must have been for her."

"Yes, but how much worse for Drake. There was no way he could follow her. He could only wait."

Natia was thinking of this conversation the following afternoon when the callers were announced. In the closed structure of society, it was not to be wondered that the Dowager Lady Devon and Lady Hartford should be acquainted, and they soon settled down to exclaim happily over the latest tidbits of scandal going the rounds. Lady Lorinda bore Lady Ellen off to see the gardens at the back of the house which were laid out in formal walks, with rose bushes and fruit trees in full bloom. Natia led Annette to a settee beside the fire and listened happily to her recitation of the doings of her offspring. A discussion of shops in the city catering to the needs of children naturally led to the question of where one could obtain the finest Brussels lace and boots of softest leather. The subject of riding apparel raised, arrangements to meet the following day for an early morning gallop were quickly settled, and Devon, coming in to take tea with the ladies, only stipulated that Riafat was to accompany them.

Had he been privileged to observe the manner in which they chose to ride, his faith in Raifat's ability to control the situation would have undergone a shock. For no sooner had they reached the Allee Verte beyond the walls of the city than they put their horses into a gallop and tore down the stretch of green beside the canal. Poor Riafat could only cast Annette's groom a look of dismay and set out in pursuit. The length of the Allee accomplished, they reined in and wheeled their mounts to retrace their steps at a more sedate walking pace.

"She is a wonderful horse," Annette remarked, running her eyes over the Arabian's points. "I do wish you could put me in the way of acquiring one."

"We plan to breed her with Colin's stallion. Perhaps we could let you have a foal."

"Are you saying he has an Arabian stallion?" Annette demanded, eyes round.

Natia realized her slip, and flushed. "Oh, dear," she murmured. "Now I've torn it."

Annette leaned forward to pat her horse's neck. "You need say no more. I shouldn't mind if you were to snub me. I deserve it."

"No, you were bound to wonder. Our honeymoon—well, it was—and it wasn't."

"Are you certain you wish to speak of this? I would hold anything you told me in strictest confidence, but you needn't, you know."

"I'm sure Colin will confide in Drake. It isn't that it is shocking—only strange, actually. I was taken by pirates at sea and sold to the Sultan of the Ottoman Empire. I would have found some means of ending my life had I been installed within the harem, but Colin rescued me before that could happen."

"Good God!" Annette exclaimed, entranced. "What an adventure!"

Natia laughed. "Indeed it was. Would you believe it, I found it great fun—after Colin rescued me, that is."

"I should rather think you did. What happened next?"

"We had five glorious weeks wandering across the desert in the company of a Bedouin tribe."

"And you acquired the Arabians from them?"

"Yes, that, and much more."

"Riafat?"

"Dearest Annette, you should have been a diplomat. Of course, Riafat. In his burnous, he stands out like a sore thumb. I wonder what tale Colin will concoct to explain him when we return to England. Something innocuous, I make no doubt."

Annette studied her profile a moment, then said, "Drake was faced with somewhat the same problem. Did Colin tell you?"

"Yes, he did. All I need to know, at least. Did you

ever wonder if there is a purpose beyond our understanding—I don't quite know how to put it."

"I know just what you mean. I have wondered about that myself. I wish we could find the answer."

They rode on for some distance without speaking, lost in thought, until Natia confided, "Living among the Turks, I could not help comparing the way they treat their women with the way ours are treated at home. There is little difference really, though we consider ourselves civilized."

"I understood they make slaves of their females," Annette remarked in some surprise.

"How many of us marry for security, or become prostitutes to support ourselves? It is only another form of slavery. I intend to establish a school where women can learn ways to support themselves."

Annette drew her horse to a halt. "But of course!" she cried. "Why didn't I think of that!"

"Would you like to help?"

"Would I ever!"

"Colin has promised space in a property he owns in London. He suggested our vicar may have ideas that will help in getting it started. But this is abominable," she added, chuckling. "We came for a pleasant morning's ride, and I have become mounted on my pet hobbyhorse."

"Well, I am now in the same case," Annette replied. "If we women do not do something about it, no one will. I have just thought of a former friend of my father. He is a retired professor, and has been looking around for something to occupy his time. It is probable he would be interested. What do you think?"

"I think it is a capital idea. To tell the truth, I did not quite know how to go about it. My dependence was all on Colin. What of Drake? Do you think he will wish you involved?"

"I am certain he won't mind, but you may be sure

I will wait to encounter him in a charming mood. Who is that Turk?"

Bewildered by the sudden change in the topic of conversation, Natia glanced around. A solitary horseman had caught Annette's attention. He was attired in proper Western dress and mounted on a roan of English breeding, and there was little in either the horse or its rider to occasion notice. As he drew near, his eyes rested for an instant on Natia's face. It was a glance so fleeting she would not have noticed had not Annette previously drawn her attention to him. As it was, she recognized his ancestry in the cast of his features and the blackness of his eyes. He passed by without giving her a second glance, and Natia dismissed him from her mind. Riafat, following a discreet distance behind, paid no heed at all to a rider who cantered past him with averted face.

Natia's enchantment with the pleasures of Brussels left little room in her mind for other considerations. She accompanied Annette on shopping expeditions, attended a concert in company with her mother-in-law, and enjoyed the treat of dining out at the finest restaurant in town. When Devon procured a box at the theater she would have preferred going alone with him, but since he was punctilious in dealing with his family, he made a point of including them in his plans.

The evening began well. Devon had gone to great plans to secure their comfort. Their box was one of the finest the theater had to offer; its occupants had a clear view of the stage, the chairs were comfortably padded, and attendants waited to pass around champagne. Natia was entranced. She had attended the theater with her parents on two occasions when visiting St. Petersburg, but had been too young to appreciate it. Never had she known anything to equal the thrill of the play unfolding before her eyes. She sat drinking in every word spoken from the stage, oblivious to everything around her until the curtain falling on the first act brought her down to earth.

Glancing idly around the house, her attention became fixed on a box on the opposite side of the theater. It was occupied by a party of an appearance so strange that many eyes were attracted to them. Indeed the man and woman in the front row seemed not to belong in the august company in which they found themselves. The woman could only be described as brassy. Her gown was obviously expensive, her hair had been dressed by an expert coiffeur, but the boldness of her glance, coupled with gestures in poor imitation of the Quality, brought the question of her antecedents immediately to everyone's mind. The man appeared in little better light. He wore a coat of exaggerated cut over a garishly embroidered waistcoat, and his pantaloons were stretched taut over a girth that could only be described as noble. He held a quizzing-glass to his eyes and was in the process of rudely surveying the countenances of the many notables in attendance at the play. Other occupants of the box stood back in the shadows, out of sight, but Natia had a fleeting impression that one of them seemed somehow familiar. It was something in the way he held his head, she thought, then put it from her mind when Thomas inquired whether she was enjoying the performance.

The Dowager Lady Devon found the spectacle of an audience more intriguing than that of actors strutting about upon a stage. One could always observe who was in company with whom, what gentleman was attempting to catch the eye of which lady. On this occasion, however, her regard was all for the people in the box across from them whom Natia had been observing. She remarked sharply on the odd creatures seen about in these uncertain times, recommended Natia pay them no heed, and subsided, saying thankfully that one would scarce expect to see their like again. The notion that she might again encounter the pair never entered Natia's head.

It was the Dowager's custom to retire to her own bedchamber each afternoon before riding out in the carriage at the fashionable hour of five. Lorinda never rested during the daytime; she had, however, awakened with the headache on the morning following the play and had not come downstairs all day. Natia partook of luncheon in the company of her mother-in-law, Devon and Thomas being from the house, then found herself alone when the Dowager went upstairs. She wandered into the salon with the vague intention of perusing a novel Lorinda had secured from the lending library, but she made slow progress. The fleeting impression of having seen the shadowy figure in the box across from them the night before kept obtruding in her thoughts. She would arrive at the bottom of a page without absorbing the gist of it, and would be obliged to start again, out of all patience with herself. She had just reread a paragraph for the third time when the butler came into the room, carefully closed the door behind him, and announced that two persons had come to call.

Something in his tone caught her attention. "Do I know them, Sudbury?" she said.

"If I may venture to say so, my lady, I doubt it. They do not appear to be of the first consequence. I took the liberty of informing them that I believed your ladyship was not at home to visitors, but regretfully they did not take the hint. They insist they have come on a matter of importance. I hesitated to show them the door without your ladyship's instruction."

"I suppose it won't hurt to see them. Where are they?"

"In the hall, my lady." A slight smile disturbed the habitually schooled impassivity of his countenance.

"I felt it imperative not to afford them an opportunity to conceal some trinket about their persons."

A delighted chuckle escaped her. "Shall we see what they want, Sudbury? Pray show them in."

"I will remain within call, my lady," Sudbury bowed and withdrew. Appearing a moment later to usher the visitors into the room, he again withdrew, leaving the door ajar.

Natia rose to her feet, in utter stupefaction to see the couple in the box across from them at the theater the evening before. Nothing of the alarm she felt could be detected in her voice. "You wished to see me?" she said.

The woman came forward with a simpering smile. On close inspection the wrinkles about her eyes and lips were clearly visible. Natia realized her face wore paint. "Do forgive the intrusion," she said, sketching a somewhat awkward curtsy. "When we saw you at the play, I thought you must be the daughter of an old and dear friend of my youth."

Natia found the encounter disconcerting. Ladies might greet each other by touching cheeks; they simply did not curtsy. The woman must surely be a servant. "Oh?" she said, and waited quietly.

"You are the image of your mother," the woman beamed, then unknowingly dropped a second curtsy.

"Indeed?" Natia murmured. "That is strange. My mother was as dark as I am fair."

The woman flushed. "I meant your face," she ventured lamely. "But we must make ourselves known to you. I am Lady—" She paused, searching for the name.

"Lord and Lady Imliff," the man finished for her, rolling forward. "When my Norma here mentioned the connection, I said we must call on you without delay."

He held out his hand as he spoke, but Natia could not bear the thought of him kissing her fingers and kept her hand at her side. After a short pause she said, "Please state your reason for coming here."

A slight frown creased his brow, but was gone on the instant. "May we not sit?" he suggested rudely, while smiling unctuously. "You are in the doldrums, but a friendly coze will cheer you up."

"No, you are mistaken," Natia replied. "I acknowledge to being busy, so if you will state your business, you can be on your way."

His beady eyes stared at her from between pockets of sagging flesh. "You will be glad we called, once you believe that Norma here and your Mum were bosom bows."

Something between amusement and indignation seized her: amusement because of their obviously rehearsed though poorly performed attempt to pass themselves off as Quality; indignation that they should presume to present themselves as acquaintances of her mother. "If you will excuse me, my butler will show you out," she said.

"Now, you lookee here," the woman cried. "We only come to give you an invite to our house."

The color rose in Natia's cheeks. "I regretfully decline, of course. Sudbury!"

The butler materialized in the open threshold. "Yes, my lady," he said, entering with two grooms close upon his heels. "If you will step this way," he said to the visitors, his tone brooking no refusal.

"Well!" the woman said. "I never seen the like! Call yourselves the gentry, do you?"

Sudbury raised his brows. "Madame!" he said, motioning the footmen to station themselves beside the callers.

There was nothing left for them to do but beat a hasty retreat. Sudbury allowed himself the unprecedented pleasure of having them shown from the premises by underlings. The gesture was of course lost on the unhappy pair. His immense interest in the proceedings was marred only by an overriding fear of what Lord Devon would have to say on learning such persons had been admitted into her ladyship's presence in the first place.

Natia, sensitive to his plight, smiled and said; "We need not dwell on the complexion of the callers, Sudbury. Suffice it to say they had mistaken me for someone else."

"Thank you, my lady," he replied from the bottom of his heart. "Will your ladyship wish them followed? His lordship may find their address of interest, should they continue in their efforts to thrust themselves upon your notice."

"That is a capital idea, Sudbury. I'm glad you thought of it. By all means, have them followed."

Sudbury, a most conscientious man, found himself unable to dissimulate and did not spare himself. He recounted the visit to Devon in detail the moment his lordship returned to the house. The intelligence that the callers had returned home to an address in an unsavory part of town made the story no more palatable, but Sudbury persevered to the bitter end. Devon was justly incensed, but with the callers, not with the butler. He knew his Natia. She could no more have turned them away without discovering their purpose than she could fly. Telling Sudbury to forget it, he went on up the stairs to Natia's room.

He found her delving into her wardrobe in an extremely agitated way. She was bent over from the waist, her head and shoulders lost to view. Devon stood appreciatively eyeing her rounded bottom, and waited for her face to reappear. Emerging with the burnous clutched in her arms that she had been wearing when she boarded the *Seahawk,* she turned, then started upon catching sight of him. "Oh!" she gasped, looking guilty. "What are you doing here?"

He strolled forward, amused. "I now require an invitation?" he said, taking her chin in his hands and depositing a kiss on the tip of her nose.

Her eyes sank before the questioning look in his. "You must wonder what I want with this?" she began, indicating the burnous.

"Anyone with a particle of sense would know you mean wearing it. May I inquire where?"

"Oh, just around," she replied vaguely.

"In that case, I need not worry," he remarked with a touch of saturninity. "I am sure you do not plan to leave the house wearing it."

She could not meet his eyes. "You have no right to come barging in here telling me what to do," she muttered in a sudden burst of temper. "I will not submit to being ridden over roughshod!"

"Dear me," he remarked mildly, seating himself in her little French chair. "We have something to hide."

"I have known from the moment I first saw you that you have not the least notion of conducting yourself as a gentleman," she shot back. "You lack elegance."

"Quite true, my love. I do. But if you imagine that I am prepared to sit idly by while you go your length, rid yourself of the notion. I am awake upon every suit."

"Nothing," she said, "will prevail upon me to remain here and listen to your unjust accusations!"

"Unjust?" he murmured. "Come, now. You know as well as I that you plan to deck yourself out in that burnous and go skulking about a wretched address for all the world like some amateurish spy. The veriest turnip-head would immediately see through your disguise."

Natia was startled into an unladylike exclamation. "How dare you!" she cried, and went on to deliver herself of a lengthy indictment of all men in general, and of one gentleman in particular.

He listened with appreciation until she ran down, then said, "I admire your pluck, but my decision remains the same. The spying will be done, my dear, but not by you."

"Oh?" she said, intrigued. "By whom?"

"By someone who shall remain nameless. That sort of thing requires experience, Natia. A spy looks just like anyone else. He doesn't call attention to himself by dressing up in some noticeable costume and sneaking around street corners."

"You are the most maddening creature I have ever met!" she declared. "Why should you think I intended anything of the kind? Of course I have more sense than that! You make me sound like some stupid, flighty female. How in the world did you know?"

"I needed some explanation for your tantrum. It seemed the likeliest that came to mind."

"I still think it is a good idea."

"It is not only a foolhardy idea, it is downright dangerous. And now, my dear, you will tell me why you became so concerned."

"Concerned? Why should you think I became concerned?"

"Natia!"

"Oh, very well. If you must know, I thought a man at the theater last evening resembled a Turk I saw while riding with Annette."

"Good God! Where was he?"

"In the box with those people who called today."

"Why the devil didn't you mention this before?"

"There is no need for you to put yourself into a taking."

"Oh, yes there is!" he retorted grimly.

"I don't see that there is. Really, Colin. You are acting strangely."

"Am I, by God! Well, let me tell you, my girl, this could be more serious than you think. Does it not strike you as odd that those people should stop by with some cock-and-bull story to worm their way into your confidence? You are to leave the matter alone! Do you hear me?"

"I should imagine everyone in the house can hear you."

"Forgive me," he said more calmly. "It is just that you frighten me at times. How could you have intended—well, never mind. In the future, Natia, come to me if anything at all seems out of the ordinary. Will you promise this? I can't protect you if you refuse to cooperate."

"Colin, do you think we should go home?" she said, not answering his question.

"If you wish to, my dear."

"But I don't," she replied, looking startled. "I imagine we wouldn't stay if you thought there was any real danger."

"I don't imagine we would," he agreed.

"Good. Then we stay."

"May I inquire, my love, the reason for this cross-examination?"

She gave her enchanting gurgle of laughter. "I want to see the outcome of Paul's infatuation for Lady Grenville. He is quite bowled over, you know. Annette tells me he has taken to referring to her as Annabelle behind her back."

"That certainly is a circumstance which makes it imperative for you to join forces with Lady Agatha," he said. "You have not given me the promise I requested."

"I thought I had, but if I haven't, I do."

He accepted this with a solemnity only betrayed by a slight twitching of his lips. "Drake tells me you and Annette have hatched an expedition between the two of you."

"We thought it would be fun to ride out tomorrow to have luncheon at a village called Waterloo. Paul and Annabelle have agreed to come along."

"Matchmaking, are you?"

"Whatever can you mean, sir?" she said, dimpling. "Are you not glad to have them join us?"

He regarded her with a kindling eye. "My dear, I don't care a straw whether they do or not. What I do care about is your focusing all your attention on me."

"Don't be absurd," she said, laughing. "I shall expect you to help entertain your guests."

CHAPTER ELEVEN

The weather being fine, the entire party assembled before the house at ten o'clock the following morning. By the time Natia descended the front steps in a pale blue habit ornamented with silver frogs and braiding. the others, with the exception of Devon, were already mounted. She gathered her bridle and put her foot in his cupped hands. He threw her up into the saddle, where she easily settled herself despite the mare's dancing about and playfully trying to unseat her. With Devon's stallion it was quite another matter. The huge Arabian bucked and reared the instant he swung aboard, in an unavailing attempt to rid himself of the unwanted burden. Paul had been waxing eloquent over the good points of both Arabians, but the stallion's antics made him glad to be astride his own docile hack. He would be sure to part company with his saddle, an unthinkable thing with Lady Grenville by as witness.

They set forward with Paul and Annabelle leading the way. Natia and Annette followed close behind them, while Devon and Drake brought up the rear. The party remained together until they had passed through the south gate of the town, but Paul and

Annabelle pulled ahead when they entered the Forest of Soignes. It presented a lovely vista with the sun filtering downward through the beech trees and a gentle breeze fluttering the leaves above their heads. Natia and Annette exclaimed over the beauty of the forest, then rode on, each lost in her own reflections.

Natia stiffened suddenly, roused from her peaceful musings by the sight of a rider wending his way between the trees. Something in the way he sat his horse left no doubt in her mind of his identity. It was inconceivable his presence would be a coincidence; she halted her horse and waited for Devon to come up with her. "It is the Turk," she said, nodding toward the rider. "I am sure of it."

It would seem he had had them under observation out of the corner of his eye, for he now spurred his horse forward and vanished from view in a flurry of hooves. Natia watched him go, her imagination calling up dreadful visions of a future bedeviled by sinister persons forever appearing out of nowhere to cut up her peace. It might be exciting, but she had had enough of it. Annette and Drake naturally asked questions, and the remainder of the ride was taken up with Devon's explanation.

The village of Waterloo was located just beyond the forest. As was to be expected, the most important building turned out to be the church, a notable domed-roof structure which quite eclipsed the more humble cottages of brick and stone. Normally the traffic of the town would have consisted mainly of its residents, but in these days of impending war soldiers in the uniforms of many nations could be seen passing through on their way to Brussels with dispatches.

They rode in and made their way to the inn, gaped at by villagers who had become accustomed to seeing the military, but not civilians. Annabelle was seated on a bench before the building, and Paul strolled through the door to watch them draw to a halt and dismount. Devon looked around and beckoned forward a young boy standing near. "Be so good as to see the horses fed and watered," he said, handing the child a coin.

" 'Pon my soul, but I'm glad we came to this devilish place," Paul said, grinning. "That fat fool inside has several bottles of the best Burgundy I ever tasted. Just wait until you roll it around your tongues."

"He should know," Annabelle said, laughing. "I dare swear he has broached every bottle in the place."

"Not a bit of it, ma'am," Paul protested, shocked. "I'm not about to uncork the port. There's four bottles of it left, and I've bought them all. One each for Drake and Devon, and two for me," he added.

"About the only attribute I have been able to discover in you, Paul, is your ability to pick a wine," Drake remarked. "Have you ordered luncheon?"

"Luncheon! If that don't beat all! Here I am telling you about the wine, and all you can think of is food!"

"Out of the way, halfling," Drake chuckled, and led Annette through the door.

"Mad!" Paul stated, holding out his arm to Annabelle. "Stark, raving mad!"

Natia and Devon trailed inside behind them, careful not to meet each other's eyes lest they give way to mirth.

Luncheon was served in the private parlour. There was a game-pie, two capons, and fish simmered in cream and flavored with herbs. By the time the meal concluded with strawberries rolled in sugar, everyone was ready to term the excursion a success. The gentlemen, well fed and therefore in benevolent frames of mind, agreed to the ladies' suggestion they visit the church, although in the normal way they might have raised objections.

Their plans were interrupted, however, when an

angry voice rose in the hall, followed by the pleading tones of the landlord. Natia, seated facing the door, looked up in time to see a tall, irate man stride by en route to the common room. He looked neither to the left nor right, and so did not perceive her shocked eyes staring out of a face that had gone dead white. One trembling hand stole to her cheek, and she cast a glance about her as if seeking a way to escape. "The Turk," she groaned, burying her face in shaking hands.

"Here?" Devon gasped, surging to his feet.

"Of course, here!" she cried, raising fearful eyes to his face. "Whatever are we to do? We must flee!"

"Where?" Devon demanded.

"The common room. No! Colin, please!" she implored, only to see him vanish through the door.

"What is amiss, Natia?" Drake asked, rising.

"The Turk has been following me for days."

"The one in the Allee Verte?"

"Yes. Oh, someone stop Colin! He will be killed!"

"What's this about a Turk?" Paul demanded, jumping to his feet.

"I know he is one of the Sultan's men!" Natia moaned, wringing her hands. "I escaped from his harem. They are after us. Oh, dear God! They won't stop until they kill us both!"

Devon, meantime, strode into the common room, his gaze coming to rest on the lone man present. "So I find you, do I?" he said, "Get up, you cur!"

The man turned his head. Yes, thought Devon. Decidedly a Turk. "Why should I?" the man replied in a voice of cold politeness.

Devon glared, his breath coming fast and short. "I'll teach you to follow Christian women! You won't live to report back to your Sultan!"

The Turk rose to his feet, knocking over his chair. "Your words puzzle me, my lord," he said softly. "I am but a poor merchant—"

"You lie!" Devon interrupted. "How do you know my title?"

"I must have heard the landlord mention it," the Turk replied smoothly, and without a moment's hesitation. His face remained calm, but he felt instinctively for his sword-hilt, then dropped his hand upon realizing he was not wearing it. He salaamed. "Another day," he said, knowing Devon had seen the movement.

"We don't require steel," Devon said through his teeth, and removed his coat. "It will be my pleasure to beat you to a pulp."

A scream from the doorway heralded Natia's arrival, and she hurled herself against Devon's chest. "No!" she shrieked. "He will have a dagger. You know he will!"

The sudden shock of her rush caused Devon to stagger. "Get her out of her, Drake," he said, gripping her by the shoulders preparatory to thrusting her away.

She clung to him like a limpet with her arms about his neck. "This has gone far enough!" she cried. "I won't have it! Do you hear me!"

Paul, who saw that Drake had no intention of intervening, cast himself into the fray. "Beast," he cried, rushing forward to aim a kick at the Turk's shins. "Enslaver of women!"

The Turk grabbed at Paul's arms to fend him off, but Drake, thinking he meant to fell Paul, ran forward and joined the assault, aiming a well-placed blow at the Turk's face. "Heathen!" he spat, kicking at his groin with all the strength he could put behind the blow.

Yelping, the Turk fell to his knees, clutching at himself. "Allah! Allah!" he moaned, rocking his body back and forth in his extreme pain.

"That's it! Call on your god!" Annette cried, running forward.

"Heathen! Spawn of the Devil!" Annabelle spat, clenching her hands into fists and advancing upon the Turk.

Drake and Paul were on them in two strides, holding them immobile with their arms about their waists. "This will never do," Drake said. "Enough! We must not kill the man!"

Annabelle kicked out and managed to land one slight blow. "That will hold him," she said smugly.

"I should rather think it would," Paul agreed, laughing down at the infuriated kitten struggling in his arms. "Oh, I say, Annabelle. It's all over. Calm yourself. Gad, but you are some woman!"

"Go to the devil," said her ladyship rudely. "You were getting all the best of it. Why did you stop?"

"If she never speaks to you again, I vow you deserve it!" Annette told him fiercely, jerking free of Drake's arms.

"Fat chance of that," Paul replied, looking at Annabelle with an odd smile lifting the corners of his mouth. "You adorable little wretch!" he added too softly for anyone else to overhear.

Their attention upon the ladies, the gentlemen failed to notice the Turk pull himself together and quietly slip from the room.

The entire staff of the inn suddenly seemed to crowd the space. The landlord and his wife, the serving-maid, and a kitchen scullery stood gaping, the landlord furiously, the maids sheepishly. The landlord held forth at length on disreputable behavior in respectable houses, but since in his excitement he reverted to his native tongue no one understood him. His wife interposed her opinions at this point, but being newly married and from Bonn, her utterances in German were equally incomprehensible to her audience.

Paul snorted and said, "Damn if I can make head or tail of what either of them is saying."

"I should imagine they wish us to leave," Devon replied in his quiet way.

"Devil a bit!" Paul exclaimed. "What will we do with the corpse?"

"My dear boy, it isn't a corpse. Not yet, at least."

"Soon will be. Makes no never mind. I say we truss him up and dump him in the river."

"I think not," Devon replied, amused. "I agree we should truss him up, but—the river, dear boy?"

Natia sighed. "I never could see why gentlemen must make such a to-do over everything," she said with a supreme disregard for the scene just enacted. "Tie him up, by all means, but put him across the back of a horse. We can question him later at home."

"You will bring a length of stout rope," Devon instructed the landlord in French. "Also a spare horse. I will pay you for it now or return it to you later, whichever you prefer. The choice is up to you. You will also present me with our bill and have our horses before the door within ten minutes."

"Certainly, my lord," the landlord bowed, anxious to see the last of his scandalous guests. "May I inquire for what purpose your lordship requires the horse? Some are for riding, and some are for pulling loads."

"This one is for riding. For our friend, the Turk."

"The Turk, my lord? He left some time ago."

"What!" Devon ejaculated, looking around. "Well, it won't do him the least good. Riafat should experience little difficulty in locating him."

Drake watched him don his coat with considerable interest. "Did Weston make it for you?" he asked.

"But of course. Some consider his work too unimaginative, but for myself I shouldn't wish my coats to announce my arrival some little time before I appear myself."

Paul broke in at this point with considerable impatience. "Damn if I see why you should choose this moment to discuss your wardrobe. We should be after the Turk."

"I have his address in Brussels, Paul," Devon explained.

"If that don't beat all!" Paul said admiringly. "How do you do it?"

"I have a resourceful wife," Devon replied without elaboration.

"This is unexpected praise," Natia commented. "A moment ago I thought you would throttle me."

"Be quiet, dear. You will give Lady Grenville a deplorable opinion of the married state."

"Call me Annabelle," that unrepentant lady laughed. "I note that others have fallen into the habit of doing so," she added, looking at Paul with amusement brimming in her eyes.

He was not proof against her smile. "Do you mind?" he said, taking her hand and leading her outside. "It doesn't matter one particle if you do, you know. I intend to keep on using it."

"Then I will be advised to accept it," she said, crossing to her horse.

He tested her girths, tightened them, and mounted her. "I too have a name, ma'am," he said, his hand lingering on her booted foot. "It's Paul."

"If you won't ma'am me, I won't sir you," she tossed at him, and sent her horse into a canter. Glancing back over her shoulder, she chuckled to see him scrambling aboard his hack, and urged her mount into a gallop.

Annette, coming out of the inn with Drake, gazed after the fast disappearing pair. "I do believe he may have met his match," she remarked. "Perhaps Annabelle will banish Judith Annis from his heart. Wretched chit! To have thrown him over the way she did!"

"That was seven years ago, my love. He was very young, and hearts do mend."

Natia, coming up with Devon, had overheard the conversation. "I did not mean to eavesdrop," she said apologetically, "but did Paul have an unhappy love affair?"

"He was engaged," Annette replied. "It was just at the time I was kidnapped; but by the time I was back home, and Paul had his Middlesex property in hand, she suddenly married an older man. Paul always claimed her father pushed her into it, but I have never been so sure. Personally I always thought he was well out of it. She was far too tame for him."

Drake threw back his head and laughed. "You can't claim that about Annabelle. She is as much a hoyden as the two of you. Eh, Colin?"

Devon appeared to give this thought consideration. "I think our ladies are too well-bred to vent their wrath on us. A handy Turk serves their purpose that much better."

"Don't let that weigh with you," Natia said, allowing him to mount her. "I feel confident Annette and I will be able to offer you enough provocation to enable you to rattle us off in prime style. Don't hesitate to do so when you feel the urge."

"The thing I most admire about both of you is your dependable habit of always having a ready answer," he commented, swinging aboard his stallion. "I might add," he grinned, "an unladylike one. Eh, Drake?"

"Go right ahead," Annette said, settling herself into her saddle. "Both of you would like nothing better than to park us in the country while you go off doing heaven knows what. Then if that didn't take the trick, you would no doubt see to it we were tied down making babies—what's so funny!"

Drake and Devon had both gone off on whoops of laughter. The landlord, drawn to the door by the sound, watched the ladies ride off sitting with their backs very stiff, and goggled to see the gentlemen trailing after them in a state of merriment. The English were either fighting duels, succumbing to hysterics, chasing after anything in skirts, or laughing their fool heads off, he thought. And that is the race which expects to defeat Napoleon, he muttered to himself, and went back inside.

It was shortly before tea time when Natia and Devon climbed the steps and entered their house to find chaos in the hall. Sudbury was admonishing the footmen toiling up the stairs bent double under the weight of a trunk to mind the console on the landing, while other footmen were collecting as many of the valises and portmanteaux as they could carry. "Were we expecting house guests?" Devon asked Sudbury, while guiding Natia around a stack of bandboxes and on past a bird cage containing a squawking parrot.

"Lady Woodham's coach arrived not ten minutes ago," the butler replied, looking harassed. "I understand your lordship's mother received word of the impending visit just this morning."

"Who is Lady Woodham?" Natia murmured, then gasped to hear the string of profanities issuing from the parrot's throat.

"Mâma's sister. Good God! Must she always travel with that damned bird? Take it away, Sudbury."

"Certainly, my lord."

"And Sudbury. It is to be kept in its cage. I won't have it flying all over the house. Remember the havoc it caused the last time Aunt Constance visited us."

"I will see that young Bert keeps it caged, my lord," he replied in a voice which gave Devon to understand that it was no fault of his that the bird had previously been allowed to escape.

"Where are they? Having tea?"

"In the drawing room, my lord," Sudbury replied, picking his way through the clutter to hold open the door for them to pass into the salon. "I will send in a fresh pot immediately."

"Shouldn't I go and change?' Natia asked, glancing down at her riding habit. "I hate to meet your relative looking like this."

"You have nothing to worry about," Devon grinned, ushering her through the door. "Wait until you see Aunt Connie!"

His mother, his sister, and Lady Woodham were seated around the tea table. Natia had been reared a lady, a circumstance which now stood her in good stead. Otherwise she might have laughed. As it was, it was all she could do to keep a straight face. Lady Woodham was on the wrong side of seventy, but dressed as a girl of twenty. She was very tall and extremely stout, and certainly should have known better. Her gown of daffodil yellow muslin was ornamented down the front with row upon row of little velvet bows —hung free from a ledge provided by her ample bosom —and clashed horribly with dyed (the color could only be described as orange) hair. A towering turban contrived of yellow silk only emphasized her height, while flounces of dainty lace around the hem of her gown made the satin slippers peeping from beneath it seem the larger.

Placing her hands on the arms of her chair, she heaved herself to her feet and surged forward to seize Natia in a somewhat violent embrace. "So you're Devon's gel?" she boomed in a voice in keeping with her size. "There now, let me look at you."

Natia found herself thrust back and subjected to the scrutiny of a pair of surprisingly keen eyes. She felt as if they bored into her very soul. Staring back, she wasn't in the least intimidated. "And you are Aunt Constance," she said. "Why haven't we met before?"

"Full of spunk, are you?" Lady Constance chuckled. "Good! It's time new blood came into this family. Been running thin of late. Sit down, child, before the tea grows cold. You, Devon! Who in hell was that Arab I saw outside in the hall?"

The Dowager Lady Devon groaned. "Constance, I must ask you to mind your language before the children! I'm sure Natia must be shocked."

"Shocked? Why should she be? She's heard the word, I'll warrant. She must have done. Anyone has who's been inside a church."

"You know she only does it to vex you, Mama," Devon laughed, going forward to seat himself beside Natia. "Why rise to the bait. The Arab is a Turk, Aunt Connie, and a very dear friend of ours. If it weren't for Riafat, neither Natia nor I would be alive today."

"Don't speak of such a thing," the Dowager implored, shuddering. "The few disclosures you made to Thomas were quite enough. I told him at the time you had no intention of giving us the truth."

"There is no need to put on your Monday face, Mama. We may have gotten ourselves into a few scrapes, but we were never bored."

"How you can speak so lightly of wandering about in company with a pack of murderous heathen, I'm sure I don't know. But that's past praying for."

"Why do so after the fact? I would hazard a guess you did not do so at the time. You hadn't the least notion there might be cause, so don't come the martyr with me."

"I know perfectly well how much you bitterly resent interference of any kind. In that respect you are just like your father, if I may scruple to say so. But, there. I am persuaded Constance will not want us discussing a topic which holds little interest for her."

"Speak for yourself, Martha," Lady Constance retorted, her eyes on Devon. "Well, sir. What hobble have you been in?"

Devon took his time responding to this and covered his silence by passing his cup to Natia. In all truth he could not make up his mind what to say. On the one hand, he knew perfectly well that his Aunt could not

be fobbed off with half-truths as his mother had; on
the other, he had no intention of confiding the de-
tails within Natia's hearing. So he compromised, saying they would discuss it later. Lady Constance was
no fool. She saw clearly that pressing the matter would
serve no other purpose than to upset her sister, and
might conceivably estrange Natia. With the calm
good sense that characterized her, she changed the
subject.

All at once the door opened and Thomas came into
the room. "You had better do something about that
parrot of yours," he informed Lady Constance, losing
no time in coming to the point. "It is loose again."

"Well, tell someone to have Bert cage it."

"He tried, Lord knows, but Mrs. Nettle chased it
with a broom. There's an unholy row going on up
there."

There was indeed. The entire staff appeared to be
gathered in the upstairs hall, all of them distracted.
Sudbury, shaken by the upheaval, wished to explain
that he had repeatedly warned Bert not to leave the
cage door ajar; the housekeeper, Mrs. Browne, delivered herself of a pungent monologue on the un-
desirability of feathered livestock flying at will through
a nobleman's home; and Lady Constance's abigail
lost no time in explaining that it was all that wretched
Bertie's fault. Devon, observing with distaste the avid
interest of the grooms and maids, cut short their en-
joyment of the drama by sending them about their
business. Before Marston could tell him the present
whereabouts of the bird, the parrot erupted from
Natia's room with Nurse and Bert in hot pursuit. The
poor creature squawked in fright at the sight of so
many hostile human faces and flew to the top of the
chandelier, well out of reach of Nurse's broom. The
dratted bird, she informed Natia, had walked all over
her best counterpane and torn the flounce of a gown
with its claws.

"If you can't control him," Devon told Bert, "I will banish him to the stables, and you with him."

Whereupon Bert burst into tears, averring he had left the cage door firmly closed, while Lady Constance and Nurse squared off to engage in a verbal encounter more raucous perhaps than the parrot. Lady Constance demanded to know by what rights Nurse had threatened her pet with bodily harm by chasing it with a broom, receiving for answer that Nurse was only interested in protecting the property of her charge and not in the outcome to the filthy bird. Bert, relieved to have attention from himself, retired into the background, and the parrot, fixing him with a beady eye, uttered a few choice phrases that were as voluble as they were profane.

Riafat, coming upon the scene, took in its meaning at a glance. Holding out his arm, he spoke soothingly in Turkish to the bird, repeating the words until the parrot ceased rocking back and forth on its perch and fluttered down to land upon his sleeve. Riafat gently stroked its feathers, handed it over to Bert, and cautioned him not to let it escape again. The staff then quietly effaced itself, Natia shooed Nurse back into her room, and Riafat salaamed and withdrew.

"Come along to my room," Lady Constance instructed Devon. "I have something to say to you."

"Yes, I thought you would," he replied, following her down the hall.

"Now, sir," she said, closing the door behind them the instant they crossed the threshold.

"Oh, Lord!" he murmured, for all the world like a rueful boy. "Where to begin?"

"This household appears to be strangely afflicted with upstart maids and foreigners creeping about the halls. What the devil does it mean? You've a madhouse here, m'boy."

"I should have warned you about Nurse. She has

been with Natia all her life, and presumes beyond her station. Ignore her. I do."

"And the Turk? Riafat, I believe you called him."

"Natia and I found ourselves in a—questionable situation. Riafat risked his life to save us, not once, but many times."

"Ran away from you, did she?"

"There had been a—misunderstanding."

"That doesn't surprise me. Natia's not your type. She couldn't have had the least notion what to do in bed."

Years before, Devon had become inured to anything his aunt might say. He fished his snuff box from a pocket. "I have always wondered why I love you," he remarked, taking a pinch between thumb and finger. "It can't be your manners; you haven't any."

Lady Constance laughed. "Don't take me wrong," she said. "I am glad you had the sense to become riveted to a decent girl."

"You would have been happy to see me marry anyone at all."

"No, you are wrong there, Devon. You are the last of the line, excusing Lorinda. She won't be breeding, poor girl. I'm not saying it's her fault, but it leaves it up to you. How'd you happen to marry Natia in the first place? I can't remember having heard anyone say."

"I do not wish to appear rude," he said, putting the snuff box back into his pocket, "but I should like to change the subject."

"Gone prickly, have you?" Lady Constance grinned. "Natia's succeeded in reforming you. Well, so much the better. My money will be in good hands."

Devon stood very still. "Indeed?" he said stiffly.

"Don't fire up at me. Everyone knows you're swimming in lard, but that doesn't come into it."

"Oh?" Devon said. "Please enlighten me."

She looked smug. "I have made you my heir."

"I fear you must hold me excused, Aunt Connie. I am not interested in your money."

"That is why I'm leaving it to you. Malcolm, God rest his soul, never had a dime, though his relatives have had the impertinence to consider that what I have is theirs. Well, it's not. It's mine, and I'll do what I damn well please with it, you may bank on that."

"Your problems with Uncle Malcolm's family have nothing to do with me. If you think I mean to stand meekly by while you—"

"Hush, Devon. You know nothing of my marriage. Malcolm made no settlements on me; hell, boy, it was the other way around. Papa settled an income on him for life, but that was all. The legal papers drawn up by Papa's lawyers insured my inheritance would belong to me."

"Let me make it plain to you—"

"It wasn't a bad marriage, as such marriages go. Oh, Malcolm had his mistresses, but that was to be expected. He was stuck with me, poor dear. You needn't look so shocked, Devon. He never pretended to a love he didn't feel, though I think he liked me well enough."

Taken aback, Devon blinked at her. "In another moment you will claim you think of me as the son you never had. It won't wash, Aunt Connie."

"For God's sake, boy, give it away if you must, but inherit it, you will."

"Leave it to Natia. She could use it for her school."

"School?" Lady Constance repeated blankly.

Devon bowed. "You will make a charming teacher," he remarked, with the glimmering of a smile.

Natia, meanwhile, in her room farther down the hall, was having her problems with Nurse. "I could wish you weren't such a goose," she said, eyeing the gown held out for her inspection. "The rent is slight. You can mend it in a trice."

Up went Nurse's chin. "I daresay I can, Missy, but that's beside the point. I won't have a nasty parrot flying about your room."

"I don't like it either, Nettle, but you choose a poor moment for making such a disturbance. Lady Constance had no more than entered the house."

"Let her stay away if she makes a practice of bringing her livestock along, is what I say."

"Well, you may find the thought wholly repugnant, but so long as Devon welcomes her, I am sure you will be constrained to accept it."

The door opened and Devon came into the room. Checking for an instant upon perceiving Nurse, he looked as though he would leave again. Dismissing her, he waited until the door closed behind her, then crossed to stand looking down at Natia.

"There seems to be little I can say," she admitted ruefully. "I have given Nettle a scold, but I don't know how much good it will do. Is Lady Constance so very angry?"

"If she became irate every time that blasted bird caused a stir, her temper would be in a perpetual state of flux. I must go to Antwerp tomorrow and remain there overnight. Will you go with me?"

"Oh, dear," she said. "I am engaged for Lady Bremman's musicale, and Annette and I promised Annabelle we would take her shopping."

He laughed and said, "By all means you must go shopping. No mere husband could expect to compete with that. You know, of course, that I have no objection to anything you may choose to buy."

"May I hold you to that?"

"Did I not say so?"

"I had thought to purchase a conveyance of some sort, Colin. The traffic is rather heavy for riding about in the coach. Do you agree?"

"I do. Your problem should not be difficult to solve. Just exercise a little judgment and I will be pleased to foot the bill."

He would have been less confident on this point had he been privileged to witness the scene taking place at the coachmaker's early the following afternoon. The three ladies had set out circumspectly enough, but by the time Natia was inspecting the various sporting vehicles on display, they had been joined by Paul and two of his friends. It was a fortuitous circumstance for him. Cantering into town accompanied by Captain Todd and Colonel Westbridge for the express purpose of calling upon Annabelle, he had perceived the occupants of Devon's town coach entering the warehouse and had followed them inside. Annabelle was enraptured by a pretty phaeton with yellow wheels, while Annette seemed taken with a curricle. Paul naturally agreed with Annabelle, but the other gentlemen felt a lady would do better with the curricle. Natia paid their assorted opinions scant heed.

Coming to a stop before an elegant high-perch phaeton, she stood gazing at it, her mind made up. "That one," she said to the manager. "I must have it."

"Dearest!" Annabelle gasped, eyeing the vehicle's huge hind wheels. "You never would! It is too unstable."

Natia smiled and shook her head. "I can manage it. I was used to drive all manner of conveyances of Papa's. I have quite decided to buy it."

"You'd better not," Paul advised. "Devon will kick up a terrible row. Isn't that so, Annette?"

"Don't look at me," Annette replied. "Devon has all my sympathy, but there is nothing I can do to stop her. I know my limitations."

"The body is hung directly over the front axle ma'am," Colonel Westbridge pointed out. "You would be quite five feet off the ground."

"And that's not all," Paul added. "Where would you get the horses?"

"I was wondering about that," Natia admitted, turning to the manager. "Where may I obtain four matched ones?"

"Natia, no!" Annette gasped. "You could never handle a phaeton-and-four!"

The manager looked as startled as the rest of them and listened to the beseechings falling on deaf ears. In his opinion, far too many ladies had taken to driving themselves about, but a phaeton-and-four for a slip of a female? A sale was a sale, however. He kept his reflections to himself and recommended an auction barn down the road.

"English gentlewomen—ha!" he barked to an assistant when, the transaction completed, Natia had departed in search of the horses, trailed by the others still protesting.

"Most ruthless females I've yet encountered," the assistant nodded in agreement.

Thus it was that Devon, guiding his stallion through the traffic en route home the following day, perceived the phaeton coming toward him at a smart trot. "Good God!" he breathed, his incredulous gaze alighting upon Natia's slender form. It was obvious that Riafat, up beside her, vouchsafed no qualms of her handling of the magnificent team of four matched grays. Devon looked thunderstruck, and then grim. Natia, catching sight of him, acknowledged his presence with a wave of her whip and swept on by without slackening pace.

Riafat, eyes carefully straight ahead, said, "Best to return home now, ladyship."

"Don't be birdwitted, Riafat," she replied. "I intend going for a turn through the park. If you fear I will overset you, say so. I will gladly put you down."

"It's his lordship's wrath I fear, ladyship," Riafat admitted. "Did you not see his face?"

"I have stolen a march on him," she laughed, featheredging a corner. "But I am tolerably certain he won't mind. You did not see any volcanic eruption, now did you?"

Riafat, who had, out of the corner of his eye, observed Devon set the Arabian forward with a plunge, now harbored no doubts about the state of his lordship's temper. He also knew he had scant hope of deterring her ladyship, and subsided, muttering something to the effect that there was nothing more to be said.

"Indeed, there isn't," Natia replied, dropping her hands slightly, allowing the grays to quicken their pace. "I may have a great many faults, but I am not lily-livered. Papa was used to say there was no stopping me, once I had taken the bit in my teeth. I suppose he was right. I was born with no nerves at all. Oh, drat! There is Lady Coreville drawn up in her carriage waiting to chat with me. Jump down, Riafat, and see what you can learn of the war in that coffee house yonder. Devon will want to know. I will take you back up in a very few minutes."

As it turned out, some twenty minutes were to pass before she was free to set the grays forward. Quitting the park, she turned into the Rue de Namur en route to the coffee house to pick up Riafat. Crowded to the curb by an approaching carriage, she dropped the team to a walk, then came to a halt as the carriage stopped abreast of her, blocking the street. Natia found herself staring incredulously into the beaming faces of the crude pair practically thrown from her home a few days previously.

"Lady Devon!" the woman cried. "How do you do! I was just telling Hubert here I was sure it was you!"

"By Jove, but you're a rattling good driver," the man added, his eyes running over her equipage, "Where'd you get them grays?"

"If you will be so good as to back your team out

of the way, I am in a hurry," Natia replied coldly.

"In a minute," the man assured her, smiling in-
gratiatingly. "I seen few females in my time with a
head for business, but you strike me as being too smart
to close your ears. You'd best hear what I got to say."

"I have no intention of doing so. Please clear the
street."

"We done learned all about you and his lordship's
doings in Constantinople and thereabouts. I fancy
your high and mighty friends would be glad to have
us tell them all we know. We could do you a lot of
harm."

"I do not frighten easily, sir, nor do I lack for
sense. Any friends of ours would be unlikely to
listen to you."

His smile faded. "I don't think you'd be wise to
risk it. You don't need to, you know. Just come to
our house for tea—"

"I would never consider it for an instant! I see I
must lay the matter of your accosting me before the
police. I should not wonder if your faces are already
known to them."

His eyes narrowed. "I think his lordship would
rather be a little friendly than have us bandy your
name about."

His threats failed to intimidate Natia. "His lordship will not be blackmailed by you any more than
I will," she said. "Your being able to find an audience
for your tales is arrant nonsense, as you very well
know. Society would be more inclined to set their
dogs on you. So pray do not talk any more foolish-
ness. I am not in the least afraid of anything you
can do. I shall, however, set up a scream if you don't
move your team out of my way."

He was shocked. Instead of displaying a decent
fear, she was evincing no alarm whatsoever. The Turk
was pressing for results, a circumstance which shook
him to the very core. The grave dug and waiting in

the garden behind their rented house would fit him just as well; if he weren't careful, he could end up in it himself. He gave an uneasy laugh. "If we could just talk this over—"

"I have become quite bored with talking to you as it is."

His gorge rose. He would have liked nothing better than to drive on, but the Turk's dark visage rose up to haunt him. "You'd better have a care," he said, driven to the point of desperation. "Take tea with us, or—"

"Ah, here comes my groom," Natia broke in. "If you value your skin, sir, you will put that sorry steed of yours in motion. Riafat just might lay hands on you."

He glared at her, but he too had observed the formidable figure picking his way through the throngs en route to join his mistress. "You haven't long to live," he spat at her, fury loosing his tongue. "Hussy!"

Natia turned her head in contemptuous disdain of watching their departure, and smiled upon Riafat. "Was there news?" she said.

"None, ladyship," he replied, climbing to the seat. "Those persons. Did they annoy you?"

"I should rather think they did," she chuckled, giving the grays the office to proceed. "Tea, indeed! As if I would!"

"They would lure you to their premises, ladyship. They mean you harm. His lordship must be told."

"Of course he must. I intend doing so immediately we arrive home."

It so happened that Devon had been in the house less than ten minutes when he heard her laugh in the hall. Striding across to the library door, he flung it open just as she was about to ascend the stairs. "If I may have a minute of your time?" he said in a tone so cold it brought her head around.

"Oh, dear," she thought as she walked past him

into the room. "The oddest thing," she began before he had opportunity for speech. "Those horrible people who called here one day—they accosted me near the park."

"I am not surprised," he said flatly. "Natia, how could you!"

"What? Oh, the phaeton. You said I could have it."

"I said nothing of the kind. Good God! Could you not have purchased something fit for a lady to drive?"

"Aren't you interested in my news?" she said, bringing him back to a topic much more to her liking. "They threatened me," she added for a topper.

His shock was all she could hope for. "Where?" he ejaculated in a strangled tone.

"Near the park. Really, Colin. I do wish you would attend to what I am saying. They invited me to tea. I refused, of course."

He grasped her wrist. "They would hardly threaten you for that! Natia, I want the truth."

"I have told you. Well, most of it, at least. First they threatened to disclose the story of our trampings across Turkey. I told them to go right ahead and talk. I did not intend to be blackmailed into putting up with their company, and anyway I knew no one would believe them."

"Dear God, I hope not."

"Why? What does it matter?"

"I shouldn't want anyone to think the Sultan had had you before I could rescue you."

"Oh!" she said. "I hadn't thought of that."

"You spoke of a threat. What was the nature of it?"

"The man said I hadn't long to live. It is nonsensical of him to think that anything could happen to me while Riafat is at hand."

He was looking at her aghast. "You haven't the least sensibility," he said.

"The man is foolish beyond belief. He doesn't worry me."

"He is a rogue, and the Turk a killer. Otherwise he would not be engaged in service to the Sultan. He won't be apt to break in here, but we will keep loaded guns handy just in case."

"We have only to go to the police—"

"With what? That you were invited to tea? Don't be contrary, my dear. Run along upstairs and let me tend to this."

"Well, but don't be long, Colin. We are due to dine with the Ardleys, don't forget."

"I will send a footman around with our regrets. You are not to leave the house, Natia, until we have caught the Turk."

"Not leave the house!" she said, surprised. "Why-ever not?"

He met her gaze unsmilingly. "In the circumstances, you must refer all decisions to me. And if you have any notion of going against my will, let me remind you I am perfectly capable of enforcing it over you."

Her hand, which was lying in her lap, clenched, but relaxed again after a moment. "There is no end to what you will say," she remarked. "Drake has told me there is no one he would rather depend on in a fix than you. Do you think I hold you in less regard?"

He seemed on the verge of some remark, but apparently thought better of it. "You know I don't mean the half of what I say when I am frightened for you," he offered in way of explanation.

"If you would explain things to me instead of or-dering me about, it would be a good thing."

"I daresay you are right. Very well. Riafat and Marston have been watching the house where the Turk is putting up. I think you may now guess it is the one rented by your questionable visitors. This is bad enough, but it is the least part of it."

She was aware of a searching expression in his eyes and said: "I know you think to spare me, but what is the worst of it?"

"The place is a veritable den of thieves. Riafat reports a continual coming and going of the most disreputable crew of cutthroats imaginable."

There came a silence while Natia thought this over. "I should imagine they may be of interest to the police, once you have caught the Turk. How do you plan to do that?"

"His movements are too unpredictable to make plans. We can only watch and wait. Eventually we will discover him alone."

"If they do not discover Riafat and Marston first. Is it not dangerous for them?"

"No one in this town pays the least heed to drunken soldiers staggering into their lodgings. It is a common enough sight."

"You have gone this far, you may as well tell me the rest. I won't be kept in the dark."

"No, I didn't suppose that you would. From the moment Sudbury first had the pair followed, I was persuaded the Turk would eventually turn up on their doorstep. It stood to reason, since you suspected him of being in their company at the theater. Marston merely donned the uniform of a Belgian rifleman and went around to rent lodgings across the street and down two doors. Riafat need only stagger in and out and with his headgear clapped down over his eyes to shield his face; not even the family who owns the house has had cause to suspect them. And now, my dear, there is no more to be said. Kindly inform Sudbury I wish to see Riafat, and Marston when he comes in."

"There is a great deal more to be said," she replied, disregarding his instruction. "Should not someone be following the Turk?"

"The hours he keeps makes it certain he is in

residence at the house. I should not be surprised to learn he pays the rent. In any event, he has been in the company of some ruffian each time he has come and gone, so it hasn't seemed wise to follow them. Now stop fretting. As I remarked before, one day he must surely be apprehended alone."

"I'm not fretting," she said, looping her arms around his neck. "At least, not over any outlandish Turk. You cannot have thought that my mind has been on anything but you."

"Most proper," he murmured, kissing her so thoroughly that she was left gasping for breath.

"Colin! Let me go! Someone is coming."

The door opened. "I have been looking all over for you, Devon. I wish to know—" The Dowager broke off, staring. "The Saints preserve us!" she said, stunned.

"It is polite to knock," he said, holding Natia firmly within the circle of his arms. "You always taught me so."

"I daresay I may have," replied the Dowager, "but this sort of thing belongs in the privacy of your rooms. Kissing Natia downstairs, indeed!"

"I agree with the part about the privacy, Mama," he said. "Close the door behind you, please."

CHAPTER TWELVE

It was not to be supposed that Natia could let the matter rest. She was actuated by the best of motives, but once she had taken an idea into her head, she found no difficulty at all in justifying it in her own mind. In Bert she found an accomplice. On the second instance of the parrot's escaping from its cage, she came to his defense and mollified the household into accepting the occurence without the excessive reaction occasioned by the bird's first bid for freedom. Convinced that the boy was innocent of negligence, she took pains to watch the parrot and was rewarded in due course by seeing it open the cage door itself by the simple expedient of reaching a claw through the bars to slide back the mechanism holding the door in place. Bert, the weight of blame lifted from his shoulders, became prejudiced in her behalf, her abject slave, in fact.

It seemed to Natia that defense must be her first object; defense meant a firearm, but how to obtain one? Those around the house were large and too unwieldy for her to manage. She wanted one that would fit into a reticule and be easy for her to fire. Enter Bert into her thinking; within the course of that same day he pressed a silver-mounted pistol into her hand, along with a box of bullets to fit it.

"Shall I load it for you, my lady?" he asked, pleased with himself and with her.

"Thank you, no," she replied. "My father taught me to shoot when I was no older than you are now. I prefer to do it for myself."

During the first three days of her confinement in the house, Annette had been her only visitor. Natia, reading in her room, looked up in delight when she appeared upon the threshold leading a child with each hand. "I thought you would take refuge up here," Annette laughed, coming forward. "Sudbury informed me Devon's mother and his aunt are entertaining Lady Sufridge in the drawing room. Formidable old biddy, isn't she?"

"I am laid down upon my bed with the headache," Natia smiled, returning her embrace. "You can only be Redding," she added, looking down upon Annette's son. "You are the image of your father."

"I am happy to meet you," he replied, minding his manners. "This is my sister, ma'am. Her name is Elizabeth, but we call her Betsy. She is only three. Say hello to the pretty lady," he added, nudging the little girl with an elbow.

Betsy dimpled. " 'Ello, pitty lady," she lisped obediently. "May I sit on your lap?"

"You certainly may," Natia chuckled, lifting the child in her arms. "There. How is that?"

"Will we eat little cakies? Redding said we would."

"Then by all means, we will," she agreed, smiling at Annette over the children's heads. "If your Mummy will ring the bell, someone will bring them in a trice."

"I hope we may have lemonade," Redding spoke up. "I don't like milk, and neither does Betsy."

"What a pair they are," Annette laughed, sitting down. "I vow I don't know what they will say next.

Drake spoils them shamefully; but then, so do I. Just shoo them away if you feel teased."

"No, no. We are doing famously, I assure you. How I envy you your children!"

"They are rather dears. I daresay you will have some of your own before long. Dearest, whatever do you mean, hiding yourself away like this? Drake either can't, or won't, tell me."

"I will explain later," Natia replied, looking up as Sudbury came into the room.

"You rang, my lady?" he said.

"Bring lemonade and little cakes for the children, please, and a pot of tea."

"I believe cook prepared both chocolate and vanilla ones just this morning, my lady," Sudbury replied, permitting himself a fleeting glance towards the two little faces gazing at him expectantly. "May I suggest the addition of a bowl of strawberries?"

Natia nodded and said with a little smile, "Most certainly the strawberries, Sudbury, I am glad you thought of it."

This approval had the effect of making the children laugh in delight, and their mother to say: "I am much afraid they are being very greedy."

"I not gweedy," Betsy piped. "I hungry. Where's the horsies?"

"We keep them in the stables. Would you like to see a parrot?"

"What's a parrot?" Betsy demanded, squirming down from Natia's lap.

"It's a bird, silly," Redding answered with the wisdom of his seven years. "It is kept in a cage."

"After you have eaten your cakes, we will take you to see him," Natia promised. "In the meanwhile, Redding, if you will rap upon that door, yes, dear, that one, I am sure my old Nurse will show you how to make paper hats."

In a twinkling it was done, and Nurse bore the

children off, beaming from ear to ear. "I don't know which of them will enjoy the treat more," Natia laughed, turning to Annette. "She has been making herself remarkable these past days. To my mind, Colin has been very nearly as trying, though he would have me believe otherwise. Tell me what has been going on in town."

"There is very little I can tell you, other than that Paul is quite smitten with Annabelle. But you know that already. Natia, dearest, whatever does this mean?"

Natia did not pretend to misunderstand. "Colin fears for my life, though what he thinks the Turk can do with people all about, I cannot tell you. Consider, too, the masses of soldiers in the neighborhood. I feel perfectly safe, but Colin will have it that that would only make it easier for someone to do me harm."

"Perhaps Drake could talk to him. I have had a riding habit made up à la Hussar in honor of Paul, and I'm dying to show it off. It is worth a try."

"It wouldn't do the least good for Drake to talk to Colin. He becomes disagreeable every time I bring the subject up. I don't mind telling you I am afraid to press him for fear he will insist on returning to England. He is of two minds about that already."

"Don't say so! It would be too dull here without you. Would you believe that the only excitement during the past two days was occasioned by two bodies being fished from the canal?"

A glint came into Natia's eyes. "Who were they?" she asked, glancing sideways at Annette.

"Lord, I don't know. Some vulgar couple, from all accounts."

"Were they by any chance lodging in the Rue de Concorde?"

"Never say you knew them!" Annette exclaimed, astonished.

"If it is the same pair, I did. I'm glad I bought a gun."

"A gun! Good God!"

Natia leaned forward to pat Annette's hand. "You are not to worry. I know how to use it."

"I don't believe you!" Annette said, staring.

"Papa taught me; you may believe he was a stern taskmaster. I always thought he regretted I wasn't born a son, though he claimed not. I used to pray at night to turn into a boy."

"You are shameless, Natia. Do you know that? Where do you keep the gun? Some safe place, I hope."

Natia got up quickly, a twinkle in her eye. "I keep it here, in my jewel case," she said, crossing to a chest. "It is the one place where Nettle would never think to pry. Yes, here it is," she added, fishing it out from under a welter of glittering gems and recrossing the room with the pistol in her hand. "It looks a bauble, but it shoots straight."

"However could you know that?"

"I tested it in the stables when no one was about. I just hope the coachman doesn't find the pellet buried in the straw and report it to Colin."

"You're running a terrible risk, Natia. He would be furious."

"Nettle is the risk. She will hang about at all the wrong times. I thought I would never get rid of her while I cleaned it. You have no idea the number of errands I was forced to invent. I'm sure she thought I had run mad."

"Surely it isn't loaded?" Annette gasped, shrinking back when Natia would have pressed it into her hand.

"Of course it is loaded, silly. Papa always said never to keep a weapon unless you are prepared to use it."

"Pray do not ask me to believe that Devon could be talked around to letting you keep it if he ever finds out. I will tell you straight out that I will not swallow that!"

"He won't know of it, for I shan't tell him. It is

just that one must be prepared for any event, however unlikely."

"Don't talk fustian to me, Natia. You would like nothing better than a set-to with a burglar. Perhaps you should have been born a man. You would put Napoleon to the rout almost single-handed. Take my advice, dearest, and put that gun away. You wouldn't want Devon to think he had a boy for wife."

A surprised look came over Natia's face and she went off on a peal of laughter which Annette soon joined. Devon, coming down the hall, heard the sounds of merriment and changed the direction of his steps. "You seem to be enjoying yourselves," he said pleasantly from the threshold.

Natia gasped and thrust her hand under her skirts. From her dismay at having him come upon the scene, and her desire to hide the gun, she became lost in a morass of half-sentences from which Annette was obliged to rescue her. Matters were not helped by Sudbury coming in at that moment with the tea tray, with Nurse and the children close upon his heels. It was enough to set her mind reeling. Surreptitiously shoving the pistol firmly beneath one silk-clad leg, she nonchalantly brought her hand forth and began to pour, then gave a little jump when Devon sat down upon the sofa beside her.

The children had placed the paper boats upon their heads and had somewhere acquired sticks. Nothing would do but that they march up and down playing at soldier, the little cakes forgotten. "Do come and have your tea," Annette said, taking Betsy by the hand. "Really, Redding, you are being naughty. Sit down, sir, this instant!"

"I wanna sit on the man's lap," said Betsy, jerking away from Annette and running forward.

"You have a charmer here," Devon chuckled, lifting her onto his knee. "In a few years Drake will have his hands full denying suitors the door."

Betsy rolled her eyes at him and stuffed a cake into her mouth. "Wanna see the horsies," she said, squirming.

Natia felt the gun slip sideways, and paled slightly. "Yes, Colin, do take the children to the stables," she said hopefully.

"I would rather see the parrot," Redding objected, and flashed his father's charming smile. "You promised."

"Indeed you will see the parrot—but after you have seen the horses," Natia replied somewhat breathlessly, fearful the gun might pop into view at any moment. "Do take them, Colin, before your tea grows cold."

His brows went up. "If I drink it first, my dear, it won't have a chance to grow cold," he remarked, his eyes on her in a way that was hard to read.

"If it does, I will send for a fresh pot," Natia insisted, aware the while of just how she must sound. "Just do not let the children near your stallion."

"Redding, you are to hold tight to Betsy's hand," Annette instructed, coming to Natia's aid. "Do exactly as Lord Devon tells you."

Devon's gaze swung from Natia to Annette and back again to Natia. His face expressionless, he tossed Betsy up onto his shoulder and took Redding by the hand. "You will like my fine stallion," he told the boy, leading him toward the door. "He is pure Arabian."

"May I sit on his back?" Redding asked, his interest caught.

"No, for he is too unpredictable. But Lady Devon's mare is gentle. You may sit on her."

"I'se up high," Betsy piped, jiggling about on Devon's shoulder and laughing down at her brother. "I'se riding on a horsie."

Annette watched them go and turned again toward Natia. "You looked quite wild there for a moment, let me tell you. I thought Devon would ask the cause."

"You may be sure he will, once he has me alone. Good God! I made certain he would see the gun."

"Well, you had better hide it, or he will be sure to. What on earth will you tell him if he does ask what was wrong?"

"I don't have the faintest notion," Natia admitted, shoving the pistol out of sight beneath her jewelry. "It will need to be some ploy I haven't tried before. You have no idea how it is to live with a man who can read your every thought."

"Oh, haven't I? I know exactly how it is. I sometimes tell Drake the truth. Why not try that now? Perhaps Devon will allow you to keep the gun after all."

"He would have it away from me on the instant."

"That might not be so bad, dearest. I would hate to hear you had accidentally shot yourself."

"Do be quiet, and help me think of some falderal to tell him. I can hardly trot out a headache for his inspection."

"Since you seem determined, there is one thing that never fails," Annette said, smiling slightly.

"If it is to work, it will need to be something—exciting."

"Gentlemen find it so," Annette gurgled. "Your bed, you goose."

Natia, it soon developed, was more than willing to accept this sage advice. The instant Devon reappeared with the children, she whisked them off to see the parrot. Going downstairs upon Annette's departure, she went immediately to the drawing room, where she endured an hour of Lady Sufridge's prosing. Her ingenuity stretched thin, she nevertheless contrived to avoid finding herself alone in Devon's company until the ladies retired to the small salon at the completion of the evening meal, leaving the gentlemen to their port. She then excused herself and went upstairs.

At the time she purchased the filmy nightgown, she had wondered if she would ever have the nerve to wear it. Of the thinnest of gauze, it was coal black, with a plunging neckline, no back at all, and slit up the sides to the waist. How shockingly erotic, she thought, slipping it on over her head. Surveying her image in the long mirror, she could not help but pink. She almost took it off, then firmed her resolve.

She hadn't long to wait. Discovering she had gone upstairs, Devon excused himself with an alacrity which brought a gleam into Lady Constance's eyes and a chuckle to her lips. Natia, on the alert, heard the sound for which she waited, and stood still, listening to his step approaching her door. Her head was bent slightly to allow the mass of glistening hair to stream freely downward over her shoulders; one leg was forward and bent at the knee, bared by the gown falling open from the waist and slipping between her thighs; the sheer fabric scarcely contained the breasts rosy in their eagerness to be out. Devon crossed the threshold and stopped dead in his tracks.

"Oh!" she said, with a great show of surprise. "You are upstairs early, dear. Are you going out?"

"What in thunder is that—that—"

"My gown?" she smiled, abandoning the pose to stroll about the room, teasing his dazed eyes. "Do you like it?"

"Stop slinking," he uttered, stunned.

"I purchased it at Madame Esteray's shop," she said chattily. "Her salesgirl told me they are much favored by Parisian courtesans. I think it is rather sweet."

Devon, his senses reeling, exerted an extreme effort and clung to the last vestige of control. "Take it off!" he said.

She opened her eyes at him. "But, dear," she said. "I have nothing on under it."

"That is obvious," he forced himself to say. "What the devil do you mean by this?"

Natia resumed her strolling. "I daresay I shall buy another one," she remarked, spinning about to send the panels of gauze swirling about her waist. "They also come in pink, and green, and red. What would you say to red?"

Devon, treated to a whirling glimpse of buttocks, stomach, and thighs, watched the fabric settle back in place, and seized her by the shoulders. Sliding his hands down her arms and inside the plunging neckline, he cupped her breasts.

"I really should not detain you," she demurred, backing off an infinitesimal amount. "If you were going out—"

"I am not going out!" he growled, grabbing her by the wrist.

"Colin," she gasped, dragged ruthlessly toward the bed. "You will ruin my gown!"

"Then you will be well served!" he retorted, snatching her into his arms and tumbling with her into the pillows. "You staged this little scene for my benefit. If I needed proof, I would have it in that wisp of fluff you have on. It barely covers your navel."

"Colin!" she uttered, shocked. "You have never talked like this before."

"You have never stirred my passions like this before," he shot back, jerking the gown down from her breasts and shoving it up to her waist. "If I hurt you, it's your own damned fault. You should have known better."

CHAPTER THIRTEEN

Natia walked into the dining room the following morning to find that Devon was not, as she had hoped, alone. The Dowager and Lady Constance were discussing the relative merits of invitations received in the morning's post, Thomas was glancing through the *Gazette de Bruxelles* with his chair pushed back from the table, and Lorinda was just in the act of pouring herself a second cup of coffee. Devon looked searchingly at Natia as she entered, and rose to push in her chair. "I was just on the point of sending someone to see if you had fallen asleep in the tub," he remarked, resuming his seat. "It is delightful to see you looking so refreshed."

Natia knew that he knew she had been soaking in hot water to banish the soreness caused by his love-making. "Thank you," she said, bristling. "Praise from so recognized a connoisseur as yourself is high praise indeed."

He smiled. "Do not be waspish, my dear," he said.

"How very odd of you," she replied. "I was being polite—in your own fashion."

The Dowager turned her lorgnette in the direction of her son. "To my mind he is excessively like his father. Dear Devereau shared the same distressing habit of twisting one's words to suit his convenience."

"Oh, I say," objected Thomas. "Can't a man eat his breakfast in peace?"

The Dowager's lorgnette became leveled at him. "You have lately fallen into the custom of uttering whatever comes into your head, Thomas. It would be more to the point for you to tell us what news you have gleaned from that wretched paper you have been perusing so diligently."

Lady Constance's chuckle greeted this remark. "In case you missed the significance of that one, Tom, Martha doesn't approve of a newspaper at table."

Thomas grinned. "Well, there isn't much in it, in any event. The French army seems to be concentrated about Maubeuge, and Sir Picton has arrived in Brussels. Don't ask me what that all means. I don't know much about army matters myself."

"Then I shouldn't think you would squander your time in reading about them," the Dowager remarked.

"I do not believe that I am prejudiced," Lorinda said, setting her cup in its saucer with a decided snap, "but if Thomas elects to read the papers, it is his own affair."

The expression of amusement on Devon's face became even more pronounced. "Shall we leave the fighting to the troops?" he inquired of the room at large.

"Pray don't be absurd," said his mother. "We were only exchanging viewpoints. And that reminds me. I will need to exchange some embroidery silks. I told Henri the greens would never match, but there was no reasoning with him. I am persuaded you will wish to oblige me, Devon; otherwise I would not venture to mention it."

It could not be said that his expression bore any resemblance to one delighted to oblige one's parent.

"I know nothing of embroidery silks, Mama. Please hold me excused."

"I am sure no mother ever had so provoking a son. You never could display the patience to allow one to complete one's thought. You will find the Turk you have been observing so assiduously at Henri's shop this afternoon at precisely three o'clock."

Devon, in the act of sipping his coffee, choked.

"Your way of going about this sorry affair fills my poor heart with foreboding," his mother continued. "Renting disreputable lodgings to peek from between slatted blinds, indeed!"

"How in God's name do you know of that?" he demanded.

"The entire household knows of it, to be sure. I beg you don't stare at me in that revolting way, Devon. Do engage to turn your eyes elsewhere."

"Bert saw Marston leaving the house dressed in a soldier's uniform, and followed him," Lady Constance explained. "Ingenious little bastard, isn't he?"

"Constance!" the Dowager Lady Devon groaned.

"Well, how would you describe the boy?" Lady Constance grinned. "As a child of unknown parentage, I make no doubt. My head gardener isn't so choosey. He just refers to him as his grandson, the—"

"Constance!" said the Dowager.

"Bert trailed the Turk to Henri's," Thómas ventured, soothing troubled waters, and tugged unhappily at his cravat. "I wanted you informed, Devon, but the ladies wouldn't hear of it."

"Males do not frequent embroidery shops," his mother-in-law informed him. "Females, on the other hand, may do so without occasioning remark. Henri was most cooperative. The Turk is to accept delivery of a gown he commissioned to be embroidered."

"It is certainly not a garment any lady of quality would wear," Lorinda added. "It is positively indecent."

"It is a mite skimpy, but I shouldn't think a man would mind," Lady Constance remarked.

"I hope, Constance," the Dowager said, "that you do not mean to compare gentlemen of our world with those of the heathen!"

"To my thinking, they are all alike."

Thomas chuckled, then found himself the recipient of a quelling look directed his way by his wife. "That may be," Lorinda admitted fairly, "but only a woman of the lowest sort would so reveal herself before her husband's eyes. But, there. We are embarrassing Natia. She is quite pink, poor dear."

"Well, I am not surprised," said the Dowager. "Really Constance, you must learn to mind your tongue. I'm sure I have said so over and over again. As for you, Devon, I have provided you with an excuse to visit the shop. I shall allow you to decide the rest. My ingenuity falls short of planning the capture for you, but you should find no difficulty in accomplishing it. When you take the trouble, you can sometimes be quite clever."

A look of amusement crept into his eyes. "Such praise, Mama, almost overwhelms me," he said.

"I will say I think it is most rude of you to take that attitude. It is no laughing matter, let me tell you. The strangest appearing people accompany the creature to the shop, though I will admit they have had the good sense to remain outside. You will need to go early, Devon, and wait within. I should imagine there is a back entrance to the place. Take your prisoner out that way."

His eyes dwelled inscrutably upon her face. "It is comforting to know the extent of your lack of ingenuity," he commented.

Lorinda, though in no way a satellite of her mother, felt moved at this point to defend her parent. "I must say, Devon, you have a knack for irritating Mama. Not but what she sometimes deserves the

things you say, it is highly improper for you to take
up a posture of disdain."

"If I have insulted Mama, I will willingly beg her
pardon."

"If?" said Lorinda. "I must be remarkably obtuse.
Does that mean you plan to follow her advice?"

"My dear sister, since this house seems to have
ears, it is safer not to reveal my plans."

"Well, if you want to know what I think," said
Thomas, "the women in this family are spoiled."

"Thomas!" Lorinda gasped, shocked to the core.

"The lot of you!" he added with a great deal of
satisfaction. "I said it at the time, and I say it now:
Bert should have gone directly to Devon."

"How true," murmured his lordship. "How dam-
nably true."

"Do not let us beat about the bush," Lady Constance
exclaimed. "If your pride keeps you from entering a
shop patronized almost exclusively by females, Martha
and I will—"

"You are very obliging, Aunt Connie," Devon inter-
jected dryly, laying down his napkin, "but I do not
propose to endanger the safety of innocent bystanders.
However much I might dislike saying it, you will all
cease meddling in my affairs. When you have finished
with your breakfast, Natia, I would like to speak
privately with you upstairs."

She rose immediately. "I am finished now," she said,
and went from the room with him.

The small clock on her mantle chimed the hour of
ten just as they crossed the threshold. "I hope you
will not bear me a grudge over last night," he said,
looking at her a little doubtfully. "I am exceedingly
sorry to have used you as I did."

"Why are you sorry?" she said, confounding him.

"I lost my head," he replied, not knowing what
else to say.

"You would not have done so if I had not flaunted myself. Do you really regret it?"

"No, but I shouldn't wish you to turn from me in disgust."

"Oh, my foolish darling," she murmured, smiling at him. "Don't you know I loved it every bit as much as you did?"

For a moment he stood gazing down into her face, then swept her into his arms. "And I was afraid I might have lost you," he uttered, kissing her.

"I never suspected you could make love like that," she said when she was able.

"Ah, but I can," he replied, kissing her again. "I'm glad you like it, for I intend repeating it."

"Well, I should hope so," she said, and gave her enchanting little gurgle of laughter. "Do you think Henri could be induced to embroider a gown for me?"

"Shameless hussy! Ladies of quality do not reveal themselves before their husbands."

"I wondered about that. What do they do?"

"They undress behind a screen, then climb into bed modestly covered from head to toe. But if I were you, my love, I would not build too much upon that bit of useless information."

"I'm glad my Mama never filled my head with such nonsensical notions. Colin, what did you really think of your mother's scheme for capturing the Turk?"

"Basically it was what I had in mind myself. Whether or not there are customers in the shop, I will instruct Henri to request he step into the back room. His friends could be watching through the windows. By the time they realize something is amiss, we will be well away."

"Your mother would have been pleased to know you shared her thinking," she reproved gently.

"You can't know my mother, sweet. She would have taken it as a license to be forever hatching plans.

Most of them would annoy you to the point of desperation. I should know. She has been busily deciding what is best for me since I can remember."

"Wretch!" Natia scolded, trying not to laugh. "Don't tell me you paid her the least heed. Of course you didn't."

"That, I own, is true," he replied, striving for a light tone. "You cast them all in the shade; every last giggling, stammering, spotted one of them."

"To talk of one's conquests is not at all the thing," she said, but with what he could only feel to be a tepid interest. "What will you do with the Turk?"

"Bring him to the stables here for questioning. I want to know if other agents of the Sultan have discovered our identity."

"The entire experience might be termed dreadful by most people, but, do you know, Colin, I cannot be sorry. It brought us close together."

"Yes, I know," he agreed, smiling. "We are not clear of it yet, however. I want you to keep Bert within your sight all day. The boy is entirely too precocious. What he lacks in experience, he more than makes up for in determination."

"Very well, dear. I will make sure his body does not become the third one pulled from the canal."

"How did you know there had been two others?" he asked, startled.

"Annette told me. You needn't compress your lips in that odious way. I did not explain to her whom they were. Well, run along, dear. I know you are anxious to get on with the fun."

His fingers went under her chin to tip her face up to his. "You are quite out of the common way, you know. You haven't said one word about my exercising care."

"It took a great deal of resolution on my part not to do so," she admitted, looping her arms about his neck. "I, sir, am presenting you with the picture of a dutiful wife. Since I have no choice, I must—regretfully, of course—play at being a lady."

"That is refreshing, at all events," he chuckled, kissing her. "Do not be alarmed if I am late in coming to you tonight. I will send word from the stables should I be delayed overly long. Just don't fret."

"No, I won't. I daresay I will know when you arrive."

But for all her brave show, she sank trembling into a chair when he had gone. She heard his step on the stairs as he went down, and then, after a moment, the front door closing. Out of her chair in a flash, she ran to the window in time to see him step into a strange coach, followed by Marston and Riafat. There was nothing in the shabby conveyance, nor in the rather sorry looking team pulling it, to cause anyone to more than glance at it passing by. Natia watched its progress down the street, saw it turn a corner in a direction away from the embroidery shop, and smiled. They were all become adept at intrigue.

She knew that low spirits would only aggravate the waiting, and tried not to allow herself to think about what Devon could be doing, or to speculate on the outcome. Sending for Bert, she insisted he accompany her downstairs, and set the unhappy boy to building card houses with a deck unearthed in a drawer. The Dowager, coming into the room, cautioned him to place the pasteboards on the structure with care lest the whole come tumbling down, and cast Natia a speculative glance. "You need something to occupy your time," she observed. "Bert, pull the bell and I will have the backgammon board brought in."

"No, really, I have never cared for games," Natia protested. "I thought I would settle down with a good book."

"Lord, child, never say you are bookish!"

"I daresay one can learn anything in the world from books," Natia replied, holding her temper in check.

"Well, I suppose no harm will come of it, so long as you keep it to yourself. Becoming known as a blue-stocking will put you out of fashion, my dear, and that, let me warn you, could spell your social ruin."

"I appreciate your concern," Natia said with marked politeness. "You will understand, however, that at my age there is nothing to be done to alter my unfortunate tastes."

"It is a great deal too bad. I am surprised that Devon has not taken you in hand. He was used to be such a stickler where Lorinda was concerned. But even so, I have never known him to exert himself over anyone as he does over you."

"My dear ma'am, I am his wife," Natia replied, amused.

"That is very true, but he has never before escorted the females in his family to social affairs above twice in his life. The first occurred when Lorinda made her debut, and the second was on the occasion of her nuptial ball. As it is now, spending an evening at home has become a very strange thing with us."

Natia could not feel that her mother-in-law had suffered from any lack of amusements in the past, but refrained from saying so. Having escaped the tedium of backgammon by morning callers being announced, she excused herself to the Dowager's elderly friends after a decent interval and went upstairs. Entering her room with a somewhat hasty stride, she cast a rueful look at Nurse. "Of all the prosing!" she said, shutting the door with a decided snap.

"What is it now, Missy?" Nurse asked, glancing up from laying freshly laundered underclothing in a drawer.

Natia gave an unladylike snort. "Colonel Rush may be retired from the army, but it is a little too much to suppose that he has Wellington's ear. Cross over into France to attack Napoleon on his own ground, indeed! As if the Duke would be so foolish! It was all I could do not to go off on the whoops."

"I take it morning callers are below," Nurse remarked, regarding her intently. "You needn't work yourself into a passion. Leave the war in the hands of the men where it belongs."

"With you, as always the men come first," Natia replied with a shrug of her shoulders. "Well, women are capable of performing feats of daring, let me inform you."

"Don't get on your high-ropes with me, Missy. His lordship is a fine figure of a man and better than you deserve. Here he has given you everything you want and still you can't be satisfied. Why, he never said one word over that phaeton and them horses you went out and bought. You are just mad because he didn't take you along to capture that nasty Turk. Fine sort of husband he would be to allow that!"

"The only thing I know of to your advantage is your ability with a fluting iron," Natia shot back, coloring. "Whatever do you suppose he's doing?"

"As to that, I couldn't say. Instead of pitying yourself, why don't you do something worthwhile? His lordship told you to keep young Bert beside you. He's a bright lad, Missy. Teach him his letters."

"Why, Nettle! How clever of you! Of course I will. Being able to read will make all the difference in his future. Send for him at once!"

When Bert came in, which he soon did, Natia settled him at a table before the window with paper and pen ready to his hand, and pulled up a chair beside him to begin the first instruction she had ever undertaken in her life. The lesson went off without a hitch other than that occasioned by the parrot's releasing itself from its cage and being chased down the hall by the grooms. The door to Natia's room being conveniently open, it flew within and found a perch on Bert's shoulder.

"Stop raising such a commotion and close the door," Natia instructed Nurse. "It may remain—we will keep it under observation, if you like—but do go away. Send luncheon and tea to us here, but otherwise leave us alone."

Bert, whether from a natural desire to learn, or from a fear of being banished from her ladyship's perfumed presence, applied himself diligently to the lesson, and the hours sped by. Absorbed in the intricacies of teaching, Natia failed to note the lengthening shadows in the room until a string of profanities issuing from the parrot's throat drew her attention to the sound of wheels crunching on gravel outside. A moment later she was at the window, joyous at seeing Devon descend from the coach. He was followed immediately by the others dragging the Turk to the ground. His hands were bound behind his back, and Marston and Riafat had him firmly between them, one of them on either side.

"Cor, but he's a big 'un," Bert breathed, watching Devon lead the way around the house toward the stables out back.

Natia turned her head to look down at him, suddenly recollecting his presence. "You will eliminate gutter language from your vocabulary, Bert," she said reprovingly. "The worst part of learning to read like a gentleman is to learn to speak like one. I will wash your mouth out with soap each time you forget."

"Can I watch you wash out the parrot's mouth?" the irrepressible Bert inquired, grinning from ear to ear.

"*May* you watch," Natia corrected. "May is asking permission. Can means you are able. See you remember. Now what?" she added as the parrot repeatedly flew against the window glass, squawking and cursing.

"There's someone sneaking around behind them

bushes," Bert informed her, craning his neck to peer around the curtains.

"Behind those bushes," Natia corrected automatically. Her brain felt numbed. A frown creased her brow. Her eyes blinked at the shadowy form moving stealthily around the corner of the house. They were followed, she thought, and became galvanized into action. Her mind refused to grapple with the possibility of Devon staggering backward with a ruffian's dagger in his chest. Personal danger was a consideration that did not occur to her, nor would it have deterred her if it had. In a twinkling she had fished her gun from beneath the jewels in the case and had checked it to make certain it was loaded. "You are not to leave this room," she tossed at Bert over her shoulder, and ran out into the hall.

Devon, meanwhile, having led the way into the stables, threw open the door into the tack room. "Don't cut his bonds," he cautioned as Riafat put his hand in the small of the Turk's back and sent him stumbling forward into the cluttered space.

"I would rather cut his throat, lordship," Riafat replied, then repeated the threat in Turkish.

"He speaks English as well as you and I," Devon remarked, looking at the Turk contemptuously. "Well, my friend, you have bungled your assignment. Your Sultan will take an unkindly view of your failure, unless I miss my guess."

For the first time since he had been seized in the back room of the embroidery shop, a gleam of emotion flickered in the Turk's eyes, but was gone on the instant. Shrugging, he waited.

"Do not judge him too harshly, lordship," Riafat interposed. "His father was a sweeper of stables, and his mother a whore. Begat upon a pile of dung, all he knows is to grovel in the dust and to fornicate with the she-dog."

Riafat's insults failed to bring any visible response from his quarry. The Turk stood as if carved from stone, his eyes staring straight ahead.

"Do you know," Devon observed chattily. "I do believe the poor chap is deaf. If anyone insulted my ancestry in that way, he would reckon with my displeasure soon enough. Even so, we cannot blame him, Riafat. He knows the punishment which awaits him upon his return to Constantinople."

"His return, lordship?" Riafat asked, feigning surprise. "He dare not return. He will do much better to tell you all you wish to know."

"Yes, that is so," Devon agreed. "I would then set him free."

The Turk studied him from under hooded lids. "Why should I trust the word of a Christian?" he said finally.

"My dear fellow," Devon began silkily, "my motives are at least as pure as your own. I have no intention of putting a period to your existence. That is in the hands of the Allah you worship. My own God does not sanction the taking of human life. He forbids it, in fact."

The Turk shook his head. "This I do not understand. Your God is weak, Englishman. Allah, praise his name, permits the faithful to triumph over those who would oppose his laws. You violated the property of our great Sultan, the chosen of Allah; for this you must die."

"In my country, Turk, women are not considered as property. But we are not here to argue the philosophy of religion. If you will but cooperate with me, you have nothing to fear, I promise you. You have that on the word of a Christian," Devon added with a faint smile.

"You mistake, Englishman," the Turk shot back. "I do not fear you. You have that on the word of a

Muslim," he added in his turn, also with a faint smile.

"Ah, but you fear your Sultan," Devon remarked, having the final word. "You would be a fool if you did not. Answer my questions and I will put you on a vessel bound for a new land across the seas called America. Refuse and you will be found trussed up in a sack before the gates of Topkapi Palace. The decision to throw you into the Bosporus would then be left up to your master. Choose carefully, Turk. Is it to be a new life in an alien land, or a watery death in a former one?"

"You're words are brave, Englishman, but your logic weak. Your agents would be seized the instant they set foot on Othman soil. Allah wills it."

"You are forgetting, Turk. We found no difficulty in rescuing her ladyship from under the nose of the agha kislar himself." Devon paused, his eyes resting mockingly on the Turk's face. "Have any of your countrymen other than yourself discovered our identity?"

The Turk had turned white. "Allah in his wisdom has not seen fit to disclose his secrets to you, Englishman," he said, a note of desperation creeping into his voice. "Surely you cannot expect even a lonely true believer to risk the wrath of God?"

"Thank you, Turk," Devon said implacably. "You have told me all I need to know. I have thought for some time that you were in this by yourself; otherwise I am sure that others of your kind would have been observed lurking in the background. Oh, yes, Turk. You have been under surveillance since you so foolishly attended the theater in company with your ill-assorted cohorts in crime. Their own bungling made their murders necessary from your point of view, I make no doubt. It also made it very necessary for you to act quickly, as evinced by your urgency in dealing with Henri. Embroidery that must be completed in a hurry suggested an early departure date from Brussels. Upon my learning of it, I felt a certain urgency myself. The rest was simplicity itself, believe me."

A voice from the open door interposed roughly: "It ain't as simple as ye seem to think, me lord. I wouldn't advise any of ye to make a sudden move."

Devon gave a start, and turned. A ruffian whom he judged to have escaped English justice by fleeing the country stood in the threshold, a businesslike firearm leveled at his heart. "Put that gun away, you fool," he said calmly, looking the man over from his head to his heels. "There is one of you and three of us; Riafat's aim with a knife is deadly, you know."

The ruffian nervously licked his lips. "Ye're a cool customer, ain't ye?" he said, the gun becoming unsteady in his hand.

"I am generally thought to be," Devon acknowledged in his maddeningly imperturbable way. "You might succeed in wounding me, but you would be dead before you could possibly reload."

"Ye just stand back out of the way, me lord. The Turk goes with me."

Devon stayed where he was. "Your instructions are quite without interest to me," he said in a voice that froze his listener to the marrow. "I would die before I allowed the Turk freedom to further endanger my wife's person. You will permit me to tell you to either fire that gun, or hand it over."

A dreadful premonition seized the ruffian. Clearly his lordship was insane. He looked from one face to another, undecided, and sorely rued the impulse that had brought him to the Turk's aid. The pay wasn't all that good, but it was too late to think of that now. "Would ye make yer wife a widow, me lord?" he asked, stalling for time.

"Would you make yourself a corpse?" Devon countered. "I shouldn't advise it. Hell gets rather warm at times, I'm told. You wouldn't wish murder added to your account."

"Resourceful bloke, ain't ye?" the ruffian growled, a rather sickly smile parting his lips.

"Oh, quite," Devon agreed in his matter-of-fact way. "You have backed yourself into a corner, my friend. You never should have become the Turk's hireling. That was not very wise, you know. Surely you could have found a more reliable employer."

"Ye're mad!" the ruffian uttered with conviction. "Blimey, if ye ain't! Well, me lord, all this chatter won't get ye nowhere. I'm done talking. Stand aside!"

"No, you stand aside," came Natia's voice from just behind the man's back. "Do not make the mistake of thinking I lack proficiency with a gun. At this range, I could hardly miss."

The ruffian turned his head and goggled at her. "Where'd ye come from?" he gasped. "Don't be pointing that popper at me head!"

She looked at him with scorn. "I would not try my patience, if I were you," she said. "I should hate to pull this trigger, but my finger seems not quite steady."

Devon's eyes moved over her face and back to the ruffian's. "You would do well to admit defeat," he advised in reasoning tones. "A gun in the hands of a female? Good God, man! It may offend your sense of propriety, but surrender before she shoots you accidentally!"

"Well!" said Natia. "I will have you know I never shoot by accident! Of all the things to say!"

At the sound of Devon's voice, the ruffian had turned his head toward him again and stood glaring, torn between a desire to bolt and fear that his lordship's words could prove only too accurate. Slowly his muscles bunched to fire and leap aside. At that moment Bert fortuitously darted around the door, slashing his arm with the dagger glittering in his hand. It was over in an instant. Both guns roared at once, Natia's aim true, the ruffian's deflected toward the Turk by his jerking his arm at the pain. Pitching forward, he was dead before he hit the floor, and the Turk, a surprised look upon his face, had slumped to his knees, a widening stain of red spreading across his chest. Natia uttered a shriek, but before it could die away, the Turk slumped over onto his side.

Rushing forward, Natia cast herself into Devon's arms, her tumultuous emotions finding relief in a burst of tears. "I made sure he would kill you!" she sobbed, clinging to his neck.

"I am unscathed, as you can see," he soothed. "There is nothing to cry about in that, is there?"

"No," she gulped, striving to stem her tears. "Oh, I am so thankful!"

"So am I, if it comes to that. It would appear your heroics drew quite a crowd."

They had, indeed. The family and the staff—everyone in the house, in fact—were gathered in the doorway, gaping. "Well, let us see what we can do for that unfortunate man," Lady Constance said, coming forward. "Send for medication and bandages, Sudbury, while we determine the extent of the injury."

"There can be nothing like it," the Dowager remarked, kneeling in the dust beside the Turk. "Guns and knives, indeed! For shame, sir! We will need to cut away your shirt to bare the wound. Your knife, Bert, if you please," she added, holding out her hand.

"It belongs to his lordship," Bert explained, disclaiming ownership. "I only borrowed it."

"Well, I never!" the Dowager gasped, staring at the gem-encrusted golden dagger. "Where did you get it, Devon?"

"Later!" he said in a low voice.

"Of course," she replied, and began to cut away the fabric from the wound, speaking soothingly to the Turk the while.

His eyes, glittering darkly in his gray, pain-wracked face, never wavered from her own. "You would nurse —enemy?" he managed to say when the wound was at last laid bare.

"Save your strength," she replied, smiling at him with compassion. "The bullet must be removed at once."

A ghastly smile flickered across his mouth. He was dying and everyone in the room knew it, including himself. He gasped out: "Lord Devon. I—"

"I am here," Devon replied, dropping to a knee beside him.

"You—right. I—only one—knew—"

Devon laid a hand upon his shoulder. "May your Allah receive you in paradise," he said, from the heart.

The Turk tried to smile, but his strength was ebbing fast. "Not—Sultan. Agha kislar. Sultan will—make pay—"

"I will send your body home to your family, Turk," he said, easing his passing. "You have my Christian word on it."

"May—Allah—bless you," the Turk managed to say, tried again to smile, and so died.

Devon helped his mother to her feet. "Go into the house, all of you," he said. "Riafat and I will tend to things out here. Tell Sudbury to send for the police."

Natia looked at him doubtfully. "We won't get into trouble over this?" she said.

"You may safely leave everything to me, my dear. There will be no trouble. Now go."

Natia recognized the implacable note in his voice and reluctantly obeyed.

The servants were, of course, agog. The strange events so unexpectely witnessed in the stables were on all their tongues. Natia, listening to their individual recountings of the tragedy, had scant opportunity to compose her own thoughts. To her dismay, she soon found herself a heroine. Embarrassed to be the center of so much flattering attention, she sent the staff about its business, excused herself to the family, and went upstairs.

Shortly before the dinner hour, Nurse, who had remained strangely silent on the conduct expected of a lady, announced that his lordship's step was approaching on the stairs. "Now you just put a smile on your face, Missy," she said, hurrying from the room. "His lordship has been through enough today without finding you looking glum."

Devon had arrived at the door by this time, and strolled in just in time to observe Nurse whisking herself away. "Her manners have greatly improved," he remarked, shrugging out of his coat. "I don't mean to complain, my love, but wherever did you get that gun?"

"I bought it. What did you do with the bodies?"

"The police were charmed to receive the ruffian's remains. As I had supposed, he was wanted for an endless list of crimes. What do you mean, you bought it?" he added, stripping off his shirt.

"What of the Turk?" she parried, evading his question.

"Arrangements are going forward to send his body home. The police have informed the Turkish Ambassador that he accidentally shot himself while cleaning his gun. Why aren't you undressing?"

"I have just dressed. It is nearly time for dinner."

"I ordered a cold collation sent up. By the time we are ready for it, a table will be laid in your sitting room."

She looked surprised. "You have never done that before," she said.

"I am in an—expansive mood tonight," he explained, unfastening the waistband of his trousers.

"You must be tired," she replied, accepting the breeches and laying them over the back of a chair. "I will see that you are not disturbed."

He stretched out his hand, and when she laid her own in it, raised it to his lips. "That is a becoming gown, my dear, but you will oblige me, I know."

She went off on a peal of laughter. "I must say I find your attitude excessively shocking. I made sure you would ring a peal over my head."

"I intend ringing your pretty neck. But first, my sweet, I mean to—well, you know."

"Decidedly, I know!" she gurgled. "Colin, dearest, how can you be so provoking? The thing is, I would prefer getting my scold behind me."

"Then you are doomed to disappointment," he chuckled, turning her about. "I never could understand why ladies must fasten their gowns with so many tiny buttons."

"If you weren't so impatient, Nettle would do it for you."

"You are forgetting I came very close to losing the privilege for all time," he said, pushing the dress down over her hips to the floor. "Where did you get that gun, by the way?"

"I sent Bert out to buy it for me. Do be careful, Colin. You will tear my chemise."

"Then you will be advised not to wear one. We must think of some special reward for Bert," he added, lifting her in his arms.

"And what of me?"

"You are about to receive yours," he said, lowering her gently to the bed.

Dell Bestsellers

- [ ] **CRY FOR THE STRANGERS** by John Saul $2.50 (11869-7)
- [ ] **WHISTLE** by James Jones $2.75 (19262-5)
- [ ] **A STRANGER IS WATCHING** by Mary Higgins Clark $2.50 (18125-9)
- [ ] **MORTAL FRIENDS** by James Carroll $2.75 (15789-7)
- [ ] **CLAUDE: THE ROUNDTREE WOMEN BOOK II** by Margaret Lewerth $2.50 (11255-9)
- [ ] **GREEN ICE** by Gerald A. Browne $2.50 (13224-X)
- [ ] **BEYOND THE POSEIDON ADVENTURE** by Paul Gallico $2.50 (10497-1)
- [ ] **COME FAITH, COME FIRE** by Vanessa Royall $2.50 (12173-6)
- [ ] **THE TAMING** by Aleen Malcolm $2.50 (18510-6)
- [ ] **AFTER THE WIND** by Eileen Lottman $2.50 (18138-0)
- [ ] **THE ROUNDTREE WOMEN: BOOK I** by Margaret Lewerth $2.50 (17594-1)
- [ ] **DREAMSNAKE** by Vonda N. McIntyre $2.25 (11729-1)
- [ ] **THE MEMORY OF EVA RYKER** by Donald A. Stanwood $2.50 (15550-9)
- [ ] **BLIZZARD** by George Stone $2.25 (11080-7)
- [ ] **THE BLACK MARBLE** by Joseph Wambaugh $2.50 (10647-8)
- [ ] **MY MOTHER/MY SELF** by Nancy Friday $2.50 (15663-7)
- [ ] **SEASON OF PASSION** by Danielle Steel $2.50 (17703-0)
- [ ] **THE DARK HORSEMAN** by Marianne Harvey $2.50 (11758-5)
- [ ] **BONFIRE** by Charles Dennis $2.25 (10659-1)

At your local bookstore or use this handy coupon for ordering:

DELL BOOKS
P.O. BOX 1000, PINEBROOK, N.J. 07058

Please send me the books I have checked above. I am enclosing $_____
(please add 35¢ per copy to cover postage and handling). Send check or money order—no cash or C.O.D.'s. Please allow up to 8 weeks for shipment.

Mr/Mrs/Miss_____

Address_____

City_____ State/Zip_____

8 MONTHS A NATIONAL BESTSELLER!

EVERGREEN

by

BELVA PLAIN

From shtetl to mansion—Evergreen is the wonderfully rich epic of Anna Friedman, who emigrates from Poland to New York, in search of a better life. Swirling from New York sweatshops to Viennese ballrooms, from suburban mansions to Nazi death camps, from riot-torn campuses to Israeli Kibbutzim, Evergreen evokes the dramatic life of one woman, a family's fortune and a century's hopes and tragedies.

A Dell Book $2.75   (13294-0)

Claude

The Roundtree Women

BOOK II
OF THIS SPELLBINDING
4-PART SERIES

by Margaret Lewerth

A RADIANT NOVEL OF YOUNG PASSION!
Swept away by the lure of the stage, Claude was an exquisite runaway seeking glamour and fame. From a small New England town to the sophisticated and ruthless film circles of Paris and Rome, she fled the safe but imprisoning bonds of childhood and discovered the thrilling, unexpected gift of love.

A Dell Book $2.50   (11255-9)